BABY-SITTERS LITTLE SISTER®

KAREN'S SCHOOL PICTURE

DON'T MISS THE OTHER BABY-SITTERS LITTLE SISTER GRAPHIC NOVELS!

KAREN'S WITCH

KAREN'S ROLLER SKATES

KAREN'S WORST DAY

KAREN'S KITTYCAT CLUB

ANN M. MARTIN

BABY-SITTERS LITTLE SISTER®

KAREN'S SCHOOL PICTURE

A GRAPHIC NOVEL BY

KATY FARINA

WITH COLOR BY BRADEN LAMB

An Imprint of
■SCHOLASTIC

This book is for Ashley Vinsel
A. M. M.

This book is for my friends, my unyielding
pillars of love and support
K. F.

Text copyright © 2022 by Ann M. Martin
Art copyright © 2022 by Katy Farina

Library of Congress Control Number: 2021937361

ISBN 978-1-338-76252-5 (hardcover)
ISBN 978-1-338-76251-8 (paperback)

10 9 8 7 6 5 4 3 2 1   22 23 24 25 26

Printed in China   62
First edition, January 2022

Edited by Cassandra Pelham Fulton and David Levithan
Book design by Shivana Sookdeo
Creative Director: Phil Falco
Publisher: David Saylor

CHAPTER 1

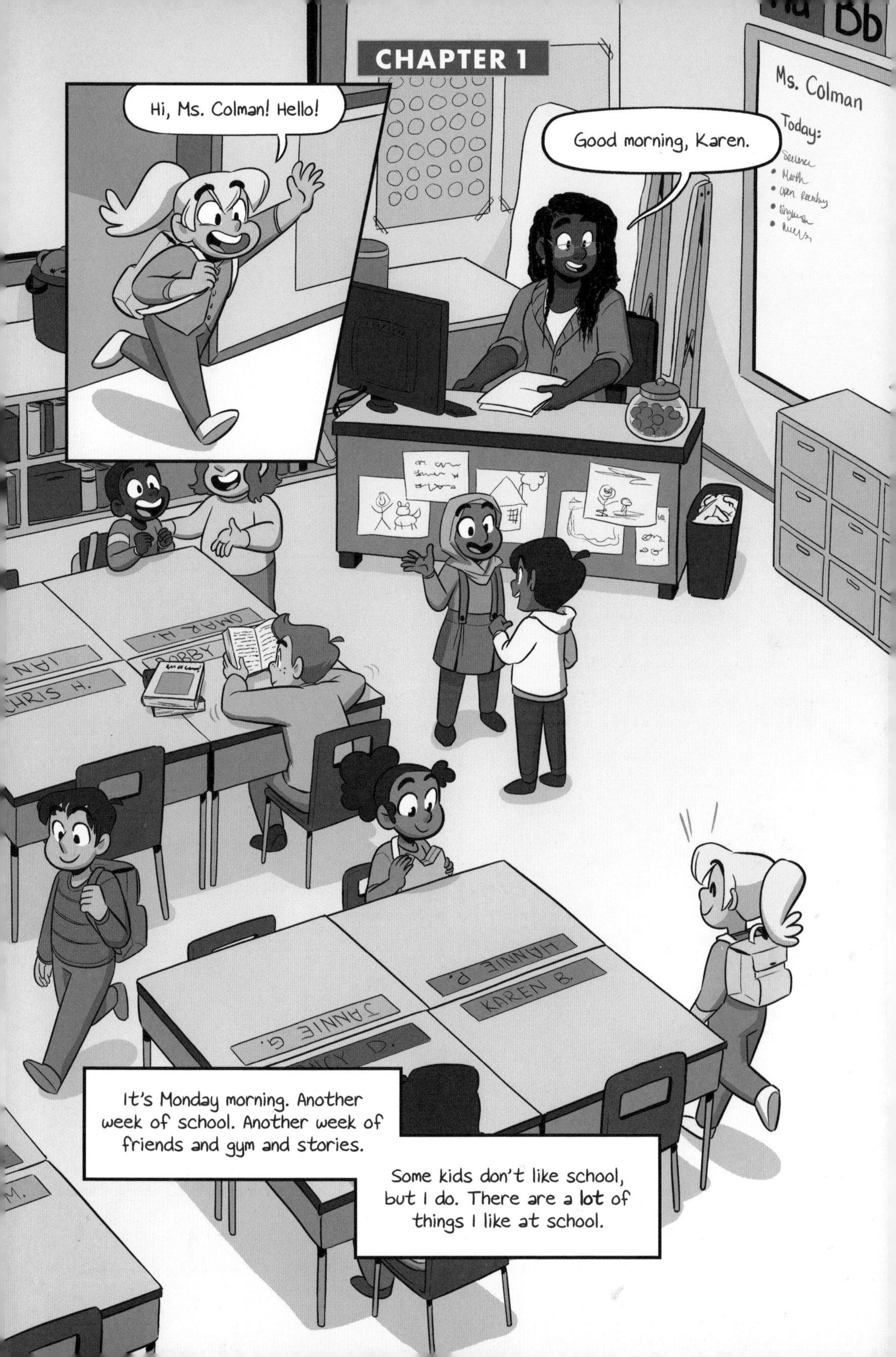

Hi, Ms. Colman! Hello!
Good morning, Karen.
Ms. Colman
Today:
OMAR H.
IAN
BOBBY
CHRIS H.
HANNIE P.
KAREN B.
JANNIE G.
It's Monday morning. Another week of school. Another week of friends and gym and stories.
Some kids don't like school, but I do. There are a **lot** of things I like at school.

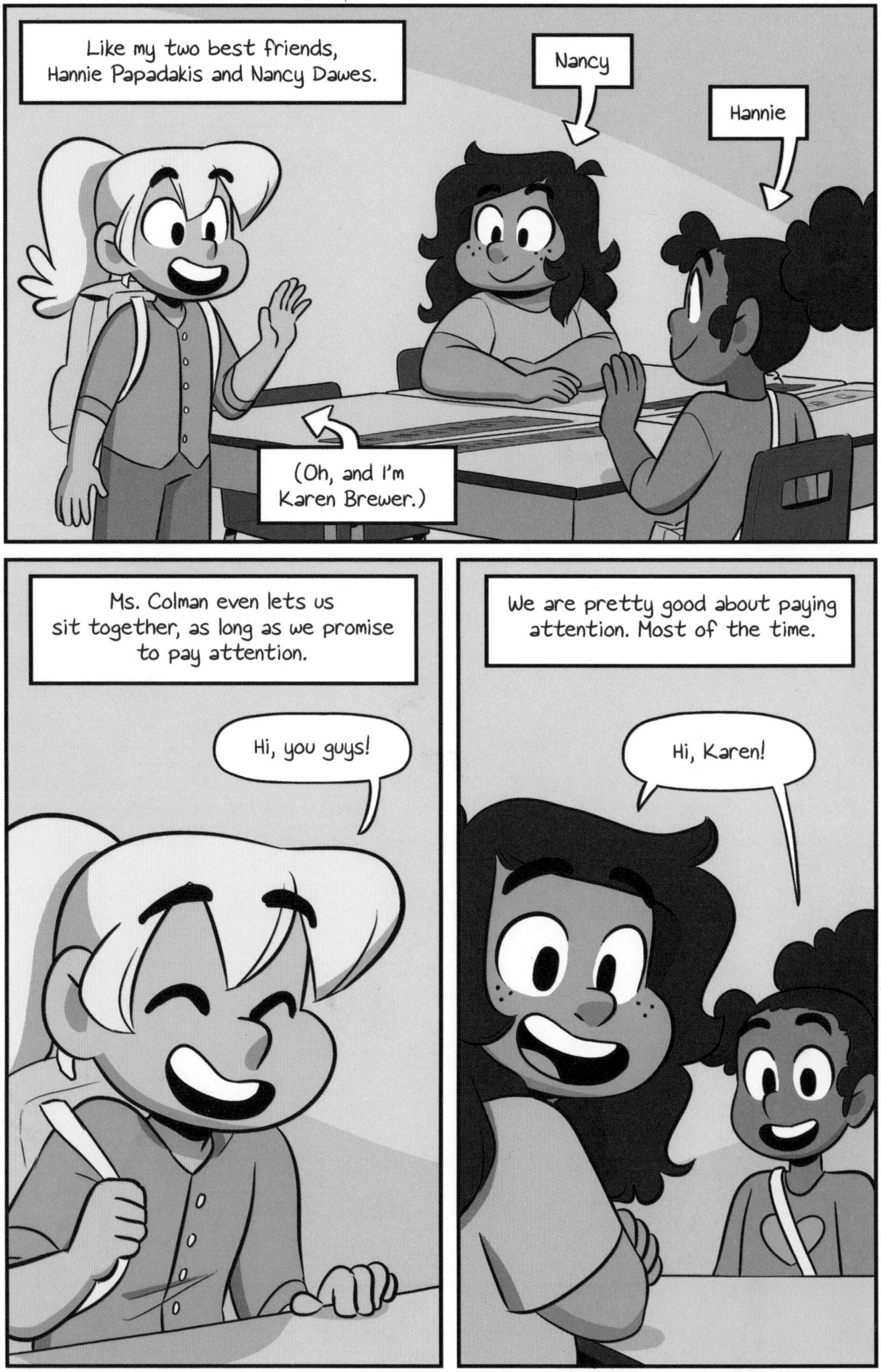
Like my two best friends, Hannie Papadakis and Nancy Dawes.
Nancy
Hannie
(Oh, and I'm Karen Brewer.)
Ms. Colman even lets us sit together, as long as we promise to pay attention.
Hi, you guys!
We are pretty good about paying attention. Most of the time.
Hi, Karen!

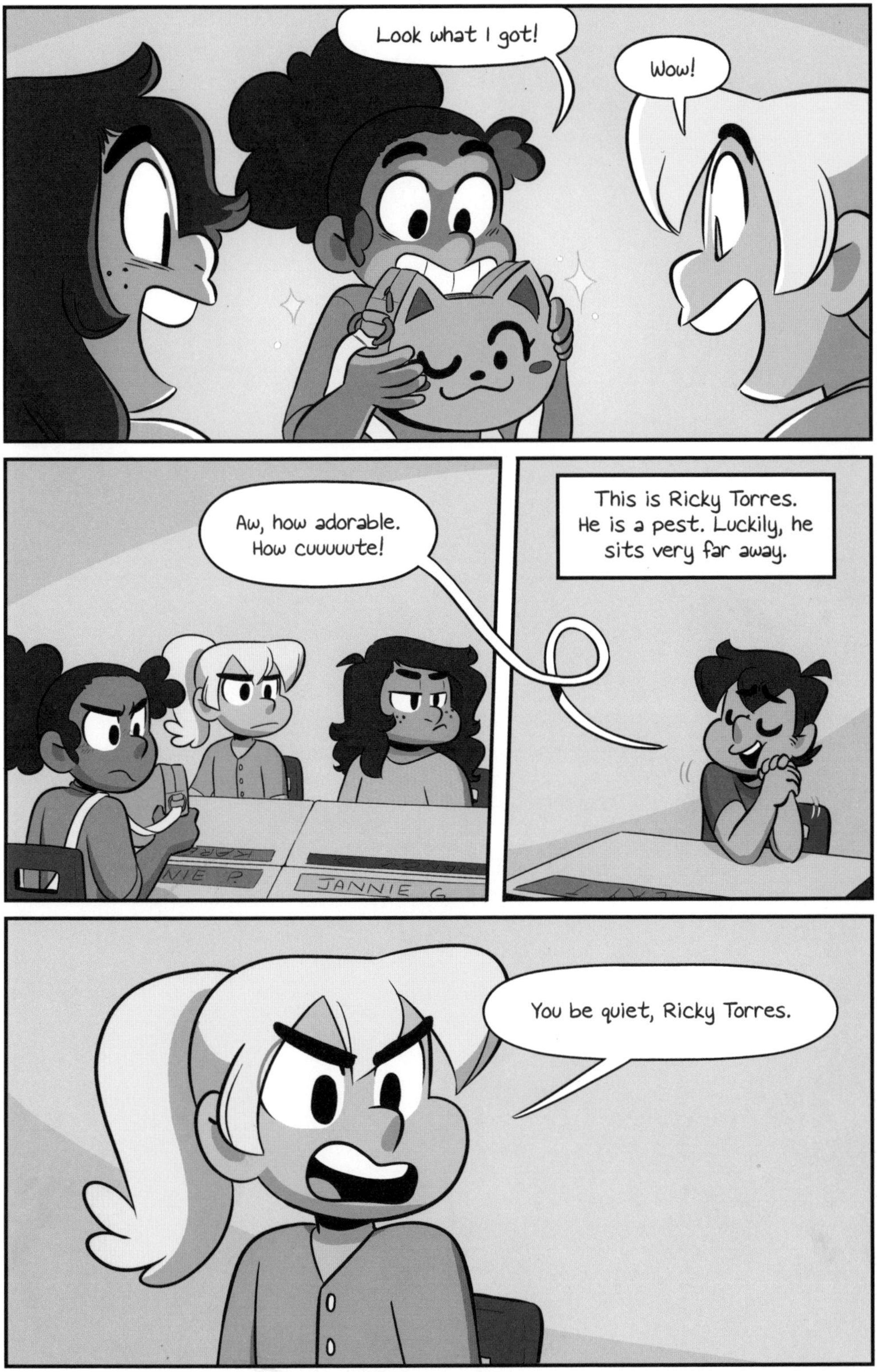
Look what I got!
Wow!
Aw, how adorable.
How cuuuuute!
This is Ricky Torres.
He is a pest. Luckily, he
sits very far away.
JANNIE G
You be quiet, Ricky Torres.

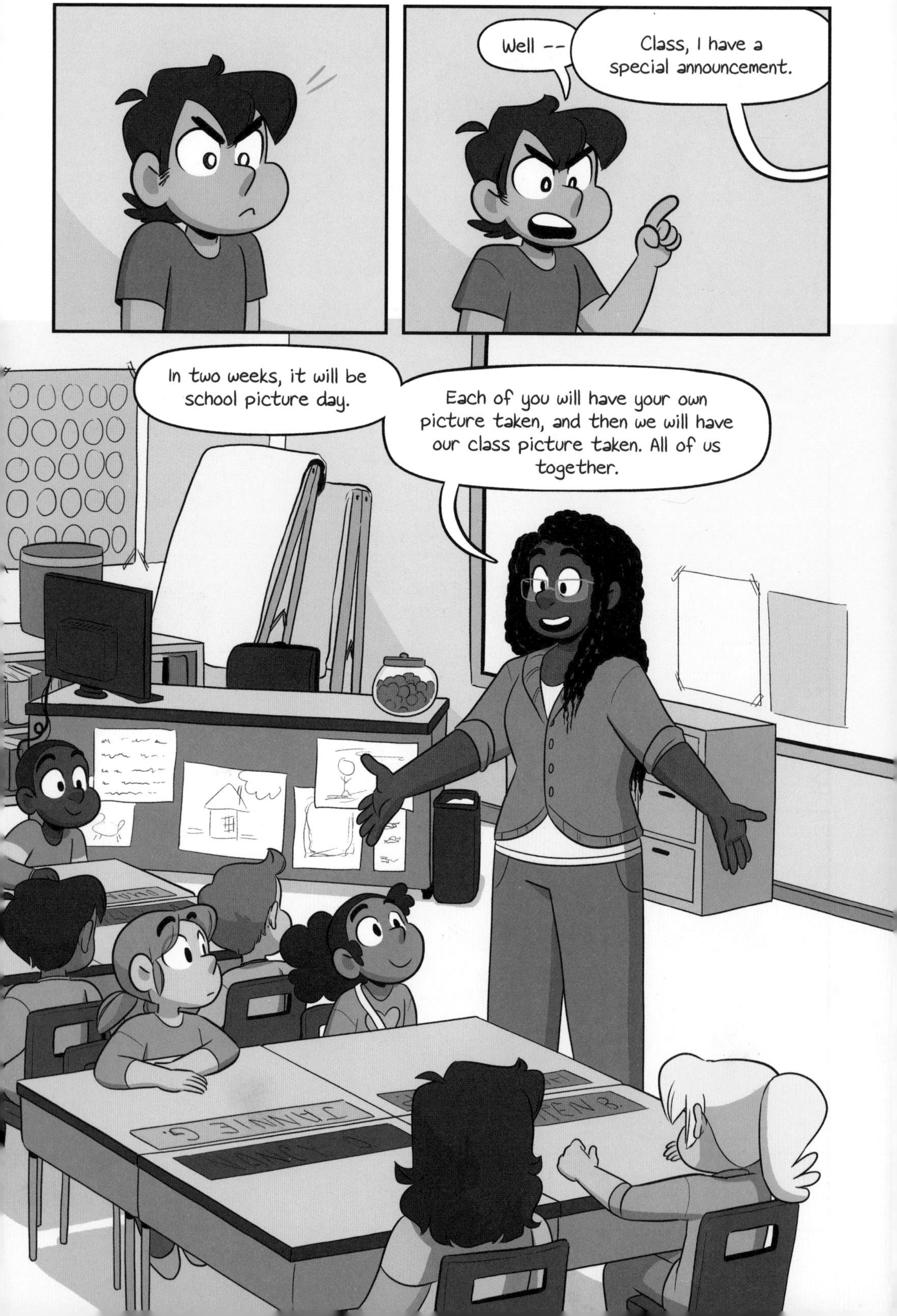
Well --
Class, I have a special announcement.
In two weeks, it will be school picture day.
Each of you will have your own picture taken, and then we will have our class picture taken. All of us together.
JANNIE G.

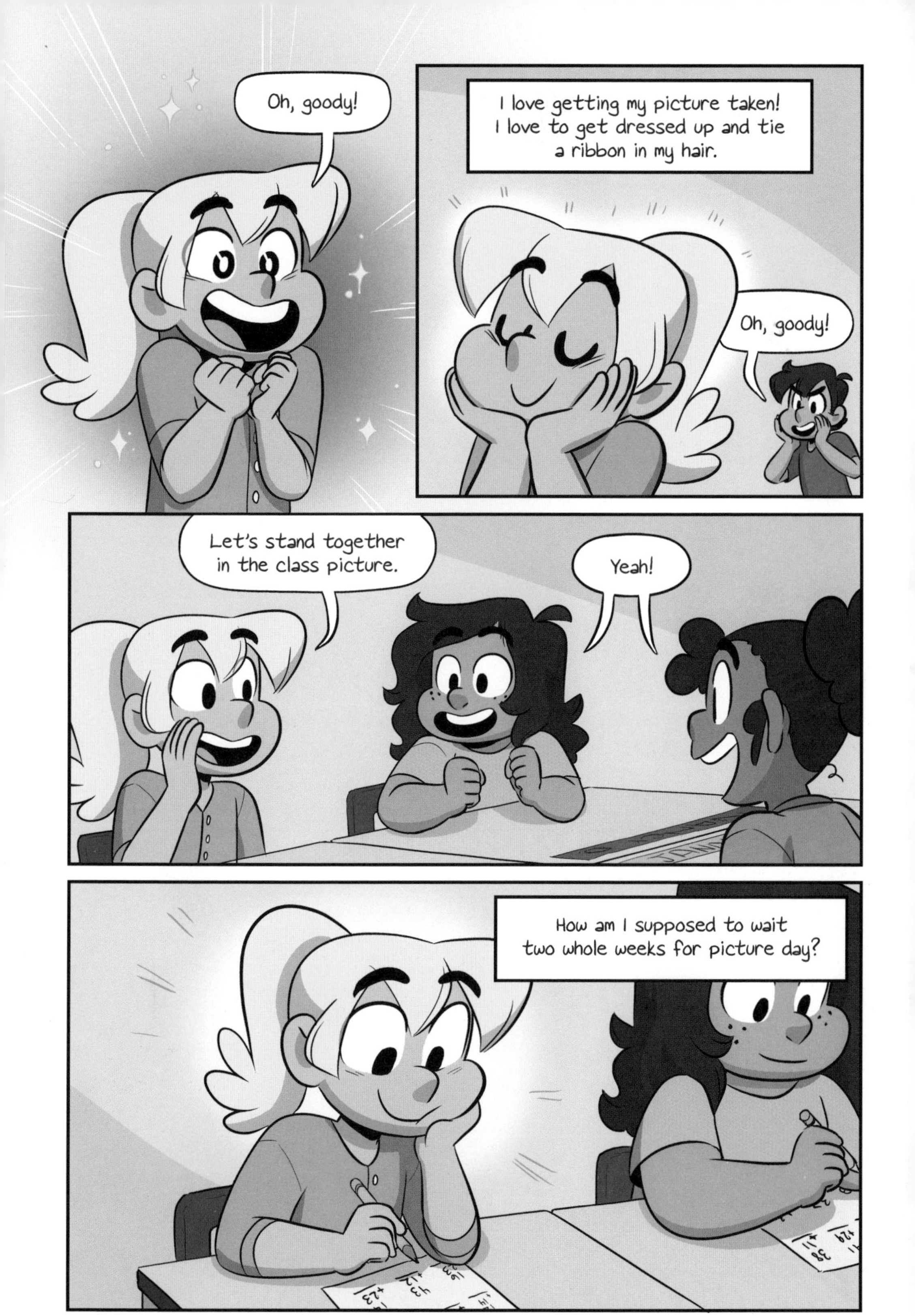
Oh, goody!
I love getting my picture taken! I love to get dressed up and tie a ribbon in my hair.
Oh, goody!
Let's stand together in the class picture.
Yeah!
How am I supposed to wait two whole weeks for picture day?

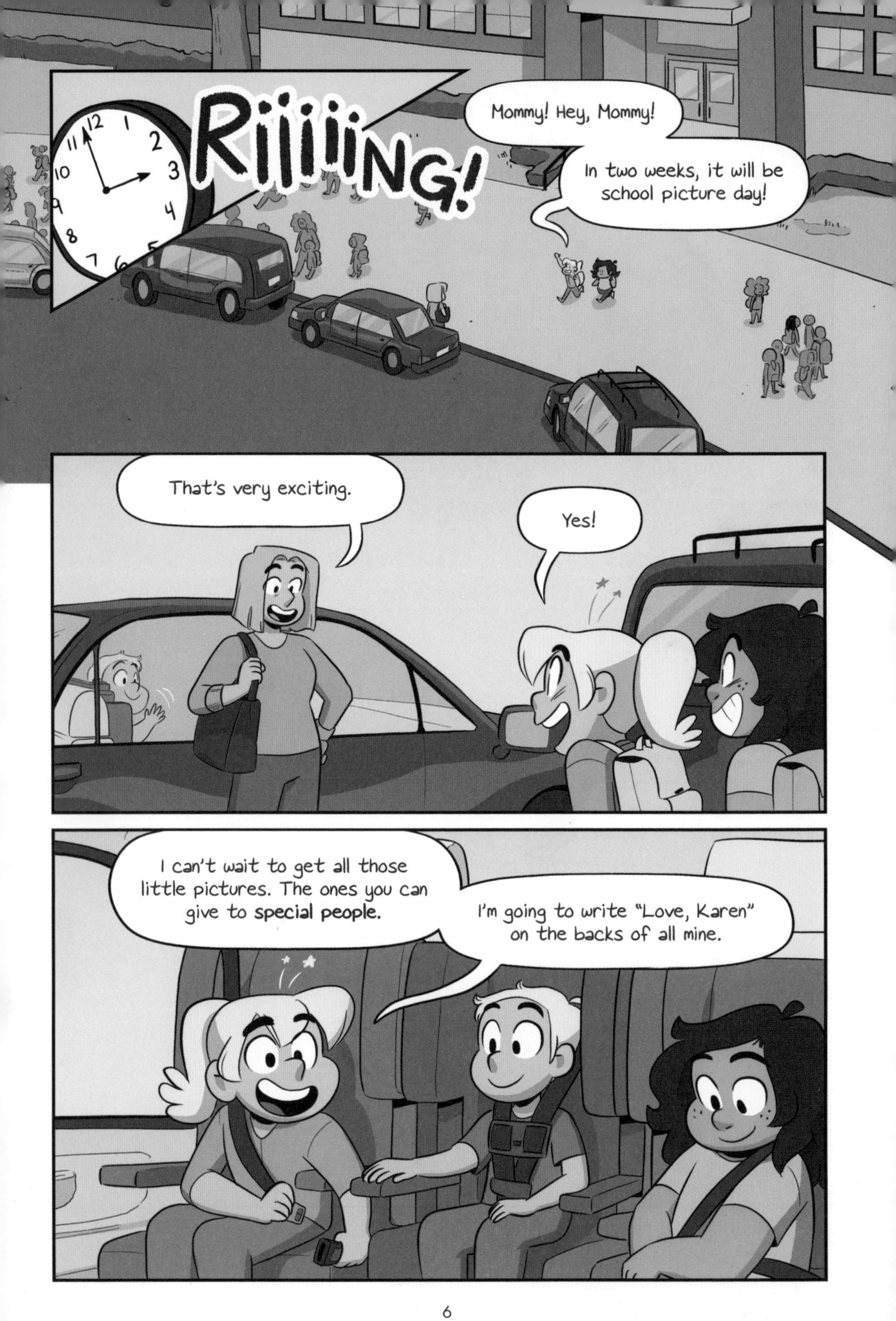

RiiiiNG!
Mommy! Hey, Mommy!
In two weeks, it will be school picture day!
That's very exciting.
Yes!
I can't wait to get all those little pictures. The ones you can give to **special people.**
I'm going to write "Love, Karen" on the backs of all mine.

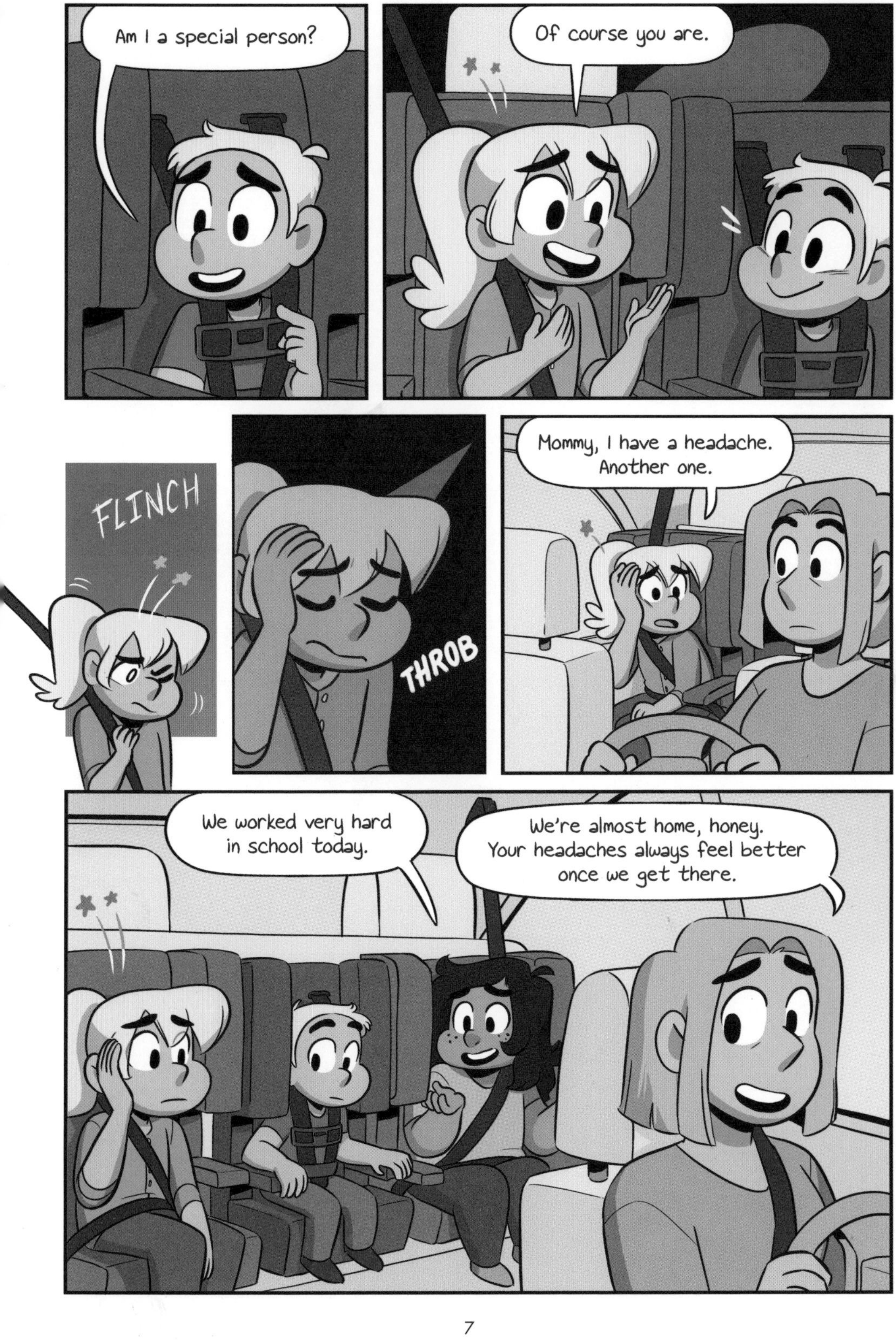
Am I a special person?
Of course you are.
FLINCH
THROB
Mommy, I have a headache. Another one.
We worked very hard in school today.
We're almost home, honey. Your headaches always feel better once we get there.

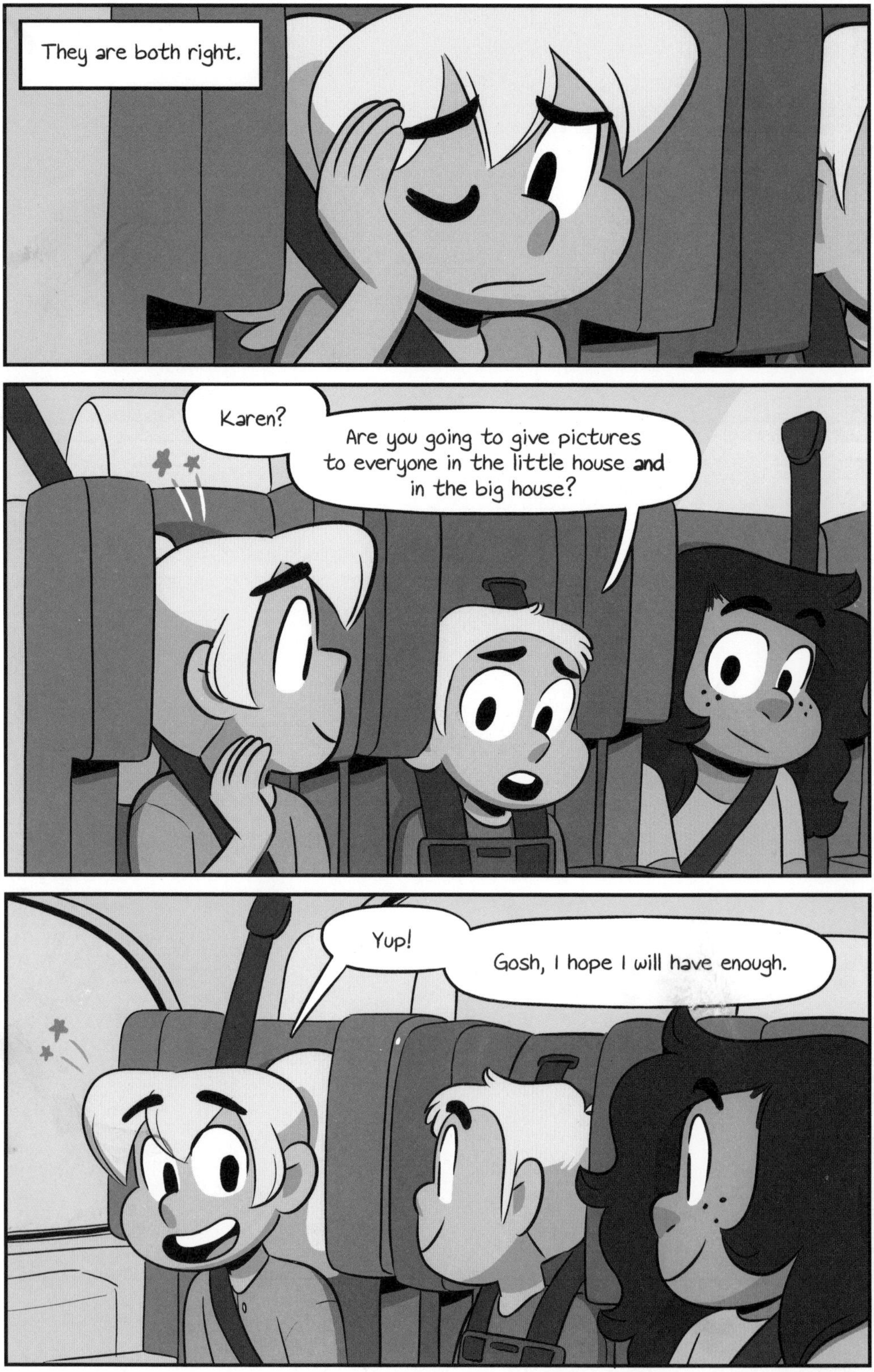
They are both right.
Karen?
Are you going to give pictures to everyone in the little house **and** in the big house?
Yup!
Gosh, I hope I will have enough.

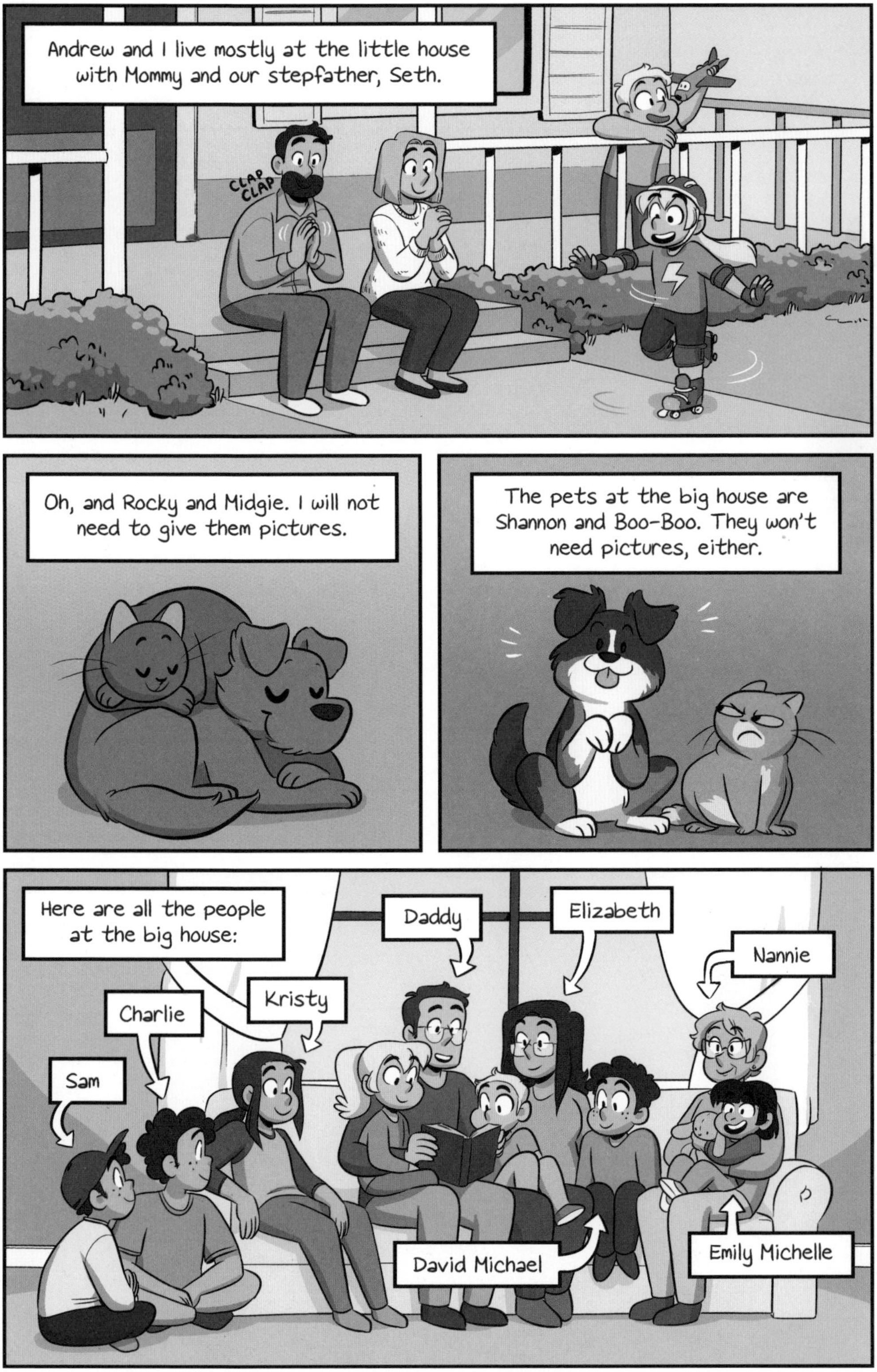
Andrew and I live mostly at the little house with Mommy and our stepfather, Seth.
CLAP CLAP
Oh, and Rocky and Midgie. I will not need to give them pictures.
The pets at the big house are Shannon and Boo-Boo. They won't need pictures, either.
Here are all the people at the big house:
Daddy
Elizabeth
Nannie
Kristy
Charlie
Sam
David Michael
Emily Michelle

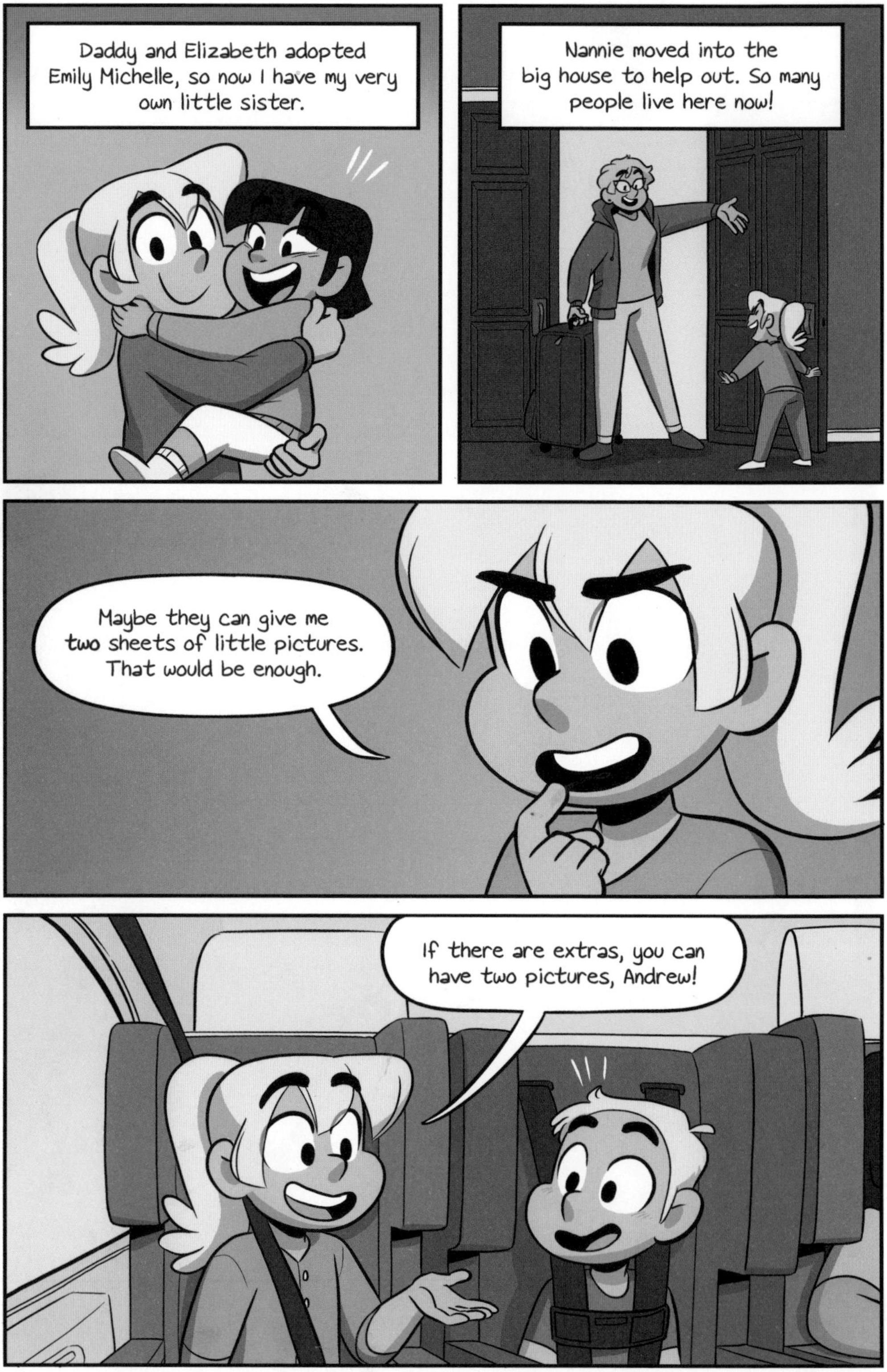
Daddy and Elizabeth adopted Emily Michelle, so now I have my very own little sister.
Nannie moved into the big house to help out. So many people live here now!
Maybe they can give me two sheets of little pictures. That would be enough.
If there are extras, you can have two pictures, Andrew!

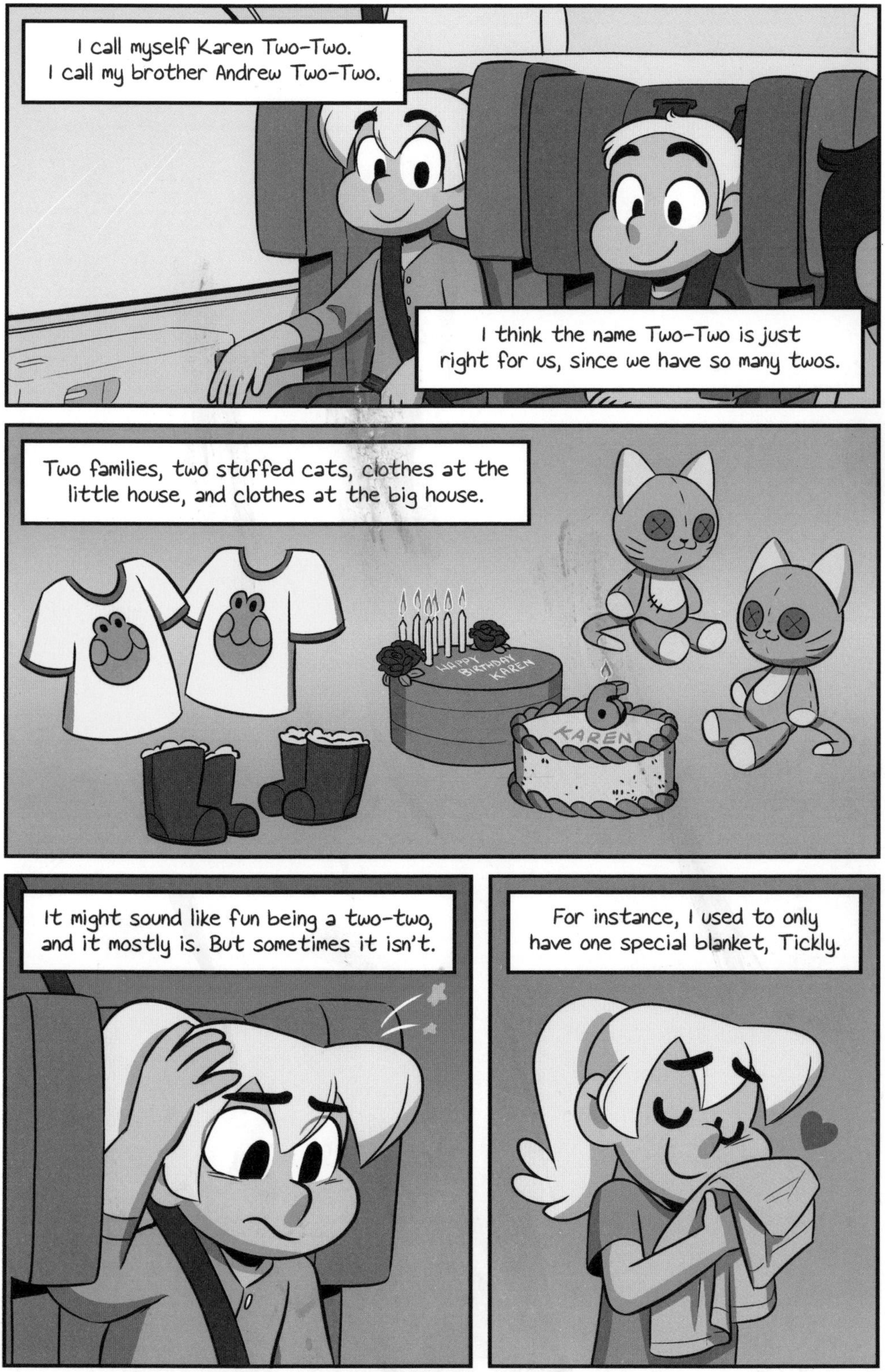
I call myself Karen Two-Two.
I call my brother Andrew Two-Two.
I think the name Two-Two is just right for us, since we have so many twos.
Two families, two stuffed cats, clothes at the little house, and clothes at the big house.
HAPPY BIRTHDAY KAREN
KAREN
It might sound like fun being a two-two, and it mostly is. But sometimes it isn't.
For instance, I used to only have one special blanket, Tickly.

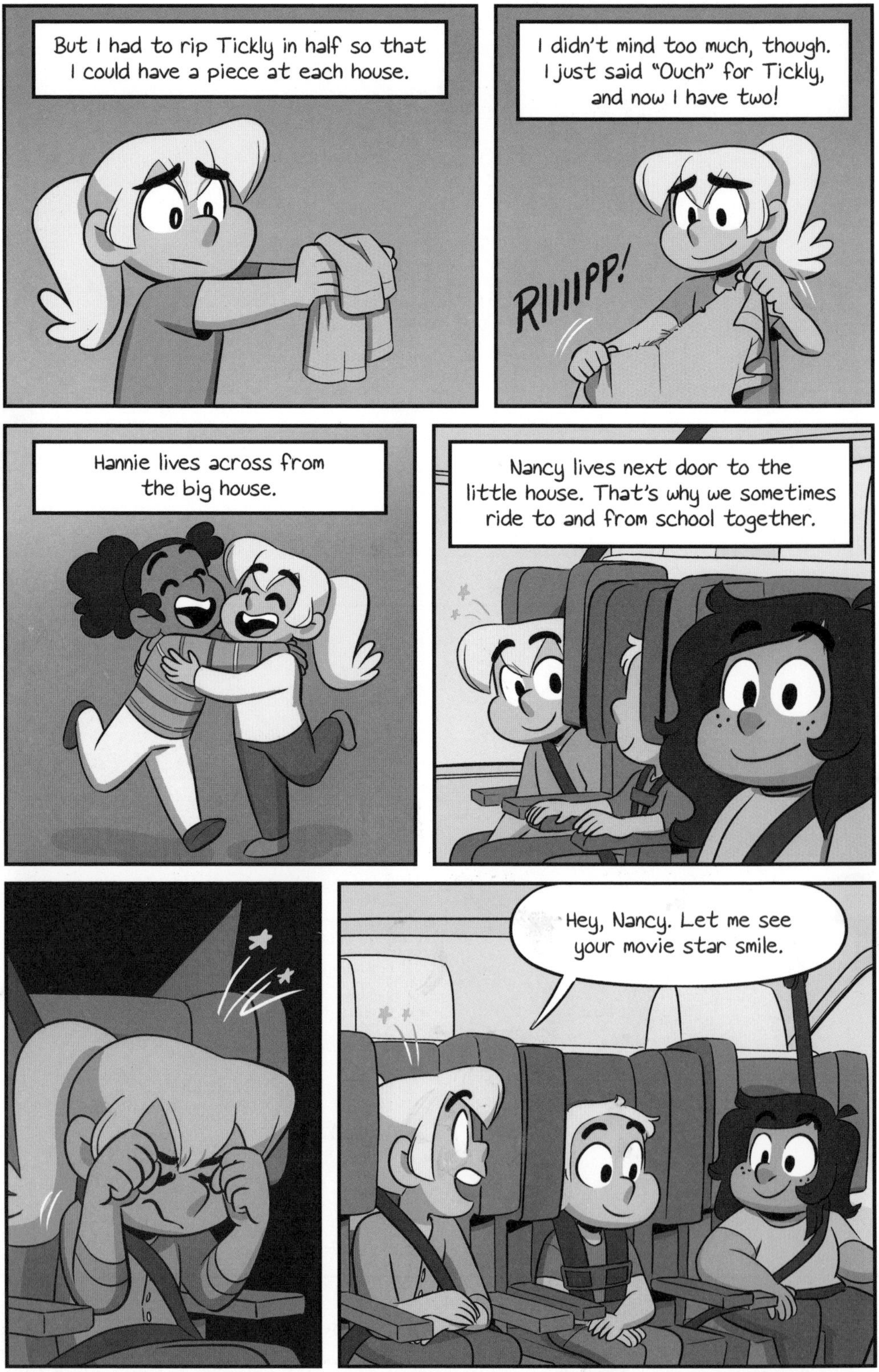

But I had to rip Tickly in half so that I could have a piece at each house.
I didn't mind too much, though. I just said "Ouch" for Tickly, and now I have two!
RIIIIPP!
Hannie lives across from the big house.
Nancy lives next door to the little house. That's why we sometimes ride to and from school together.
Hey, Nancy. Let me see your movie star smile.

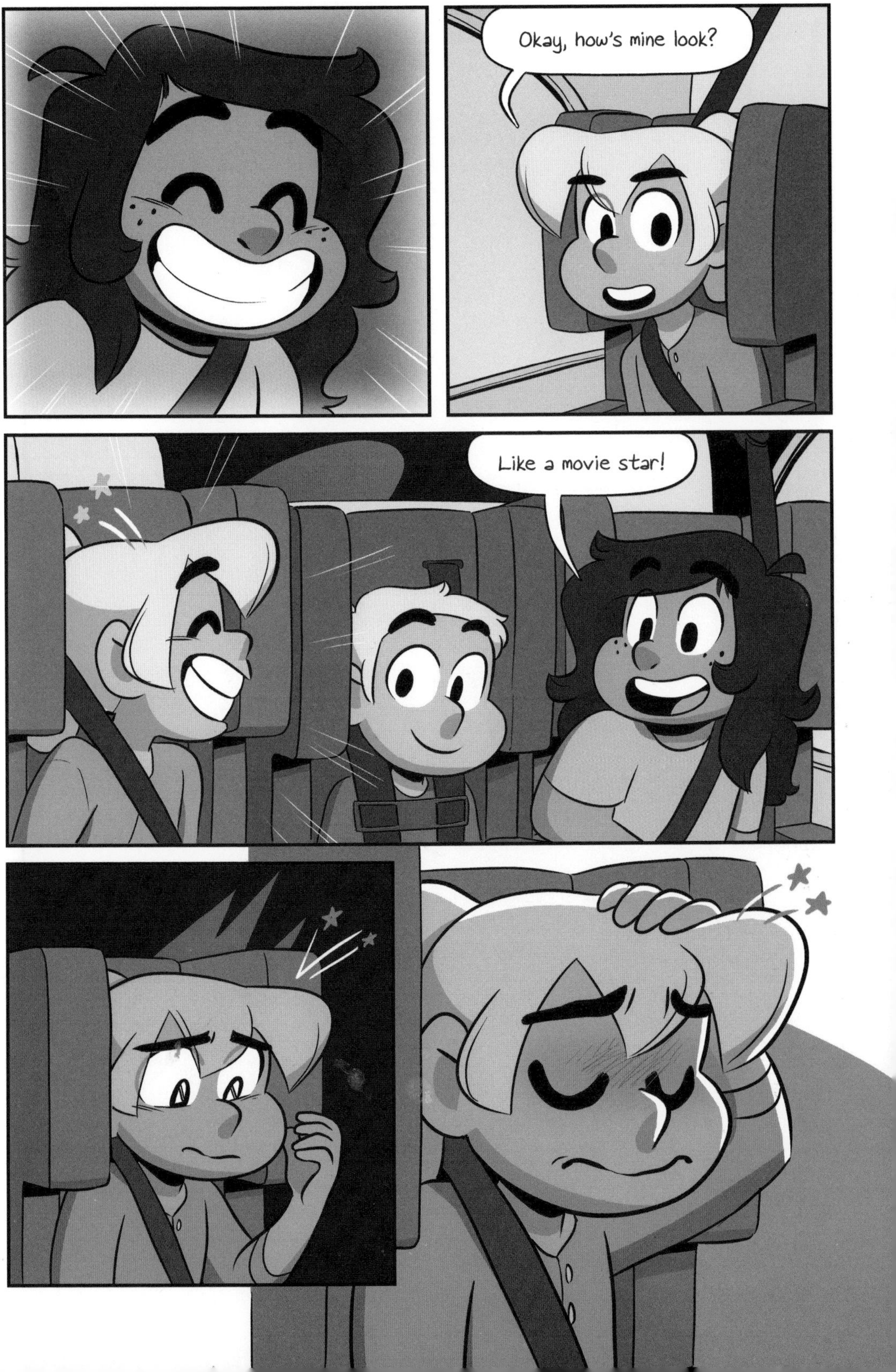
Okay, how's mine look?
Like a movie star!

CHAPTER 2

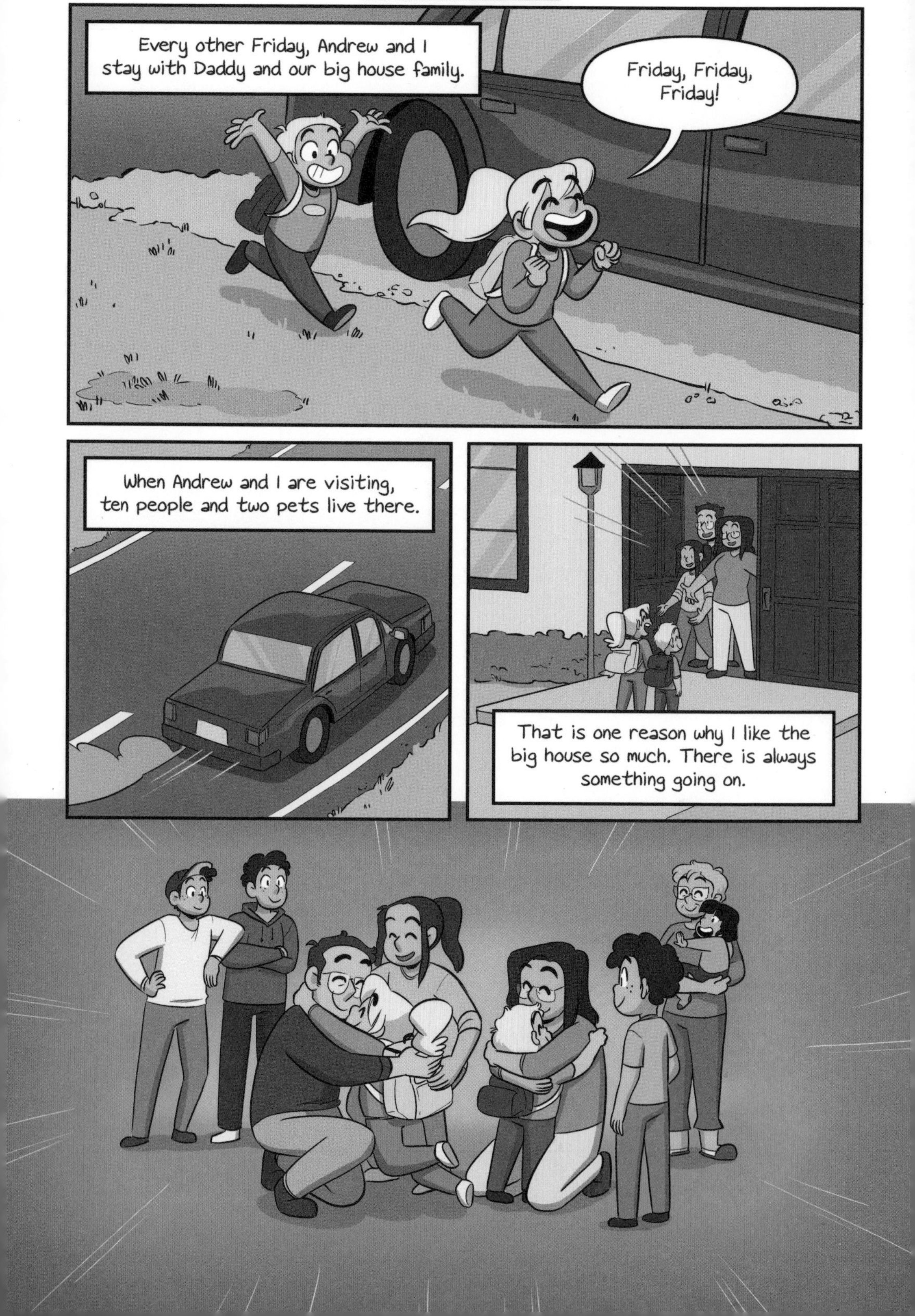
Every other Friday, Andrew and I stay with Daddy and our big house family.
Friday, Friday, Friday!
When Andrew and I are visiting, ten people and two pets live there.
That is one reason why I like the big house so much. There is always something going on.

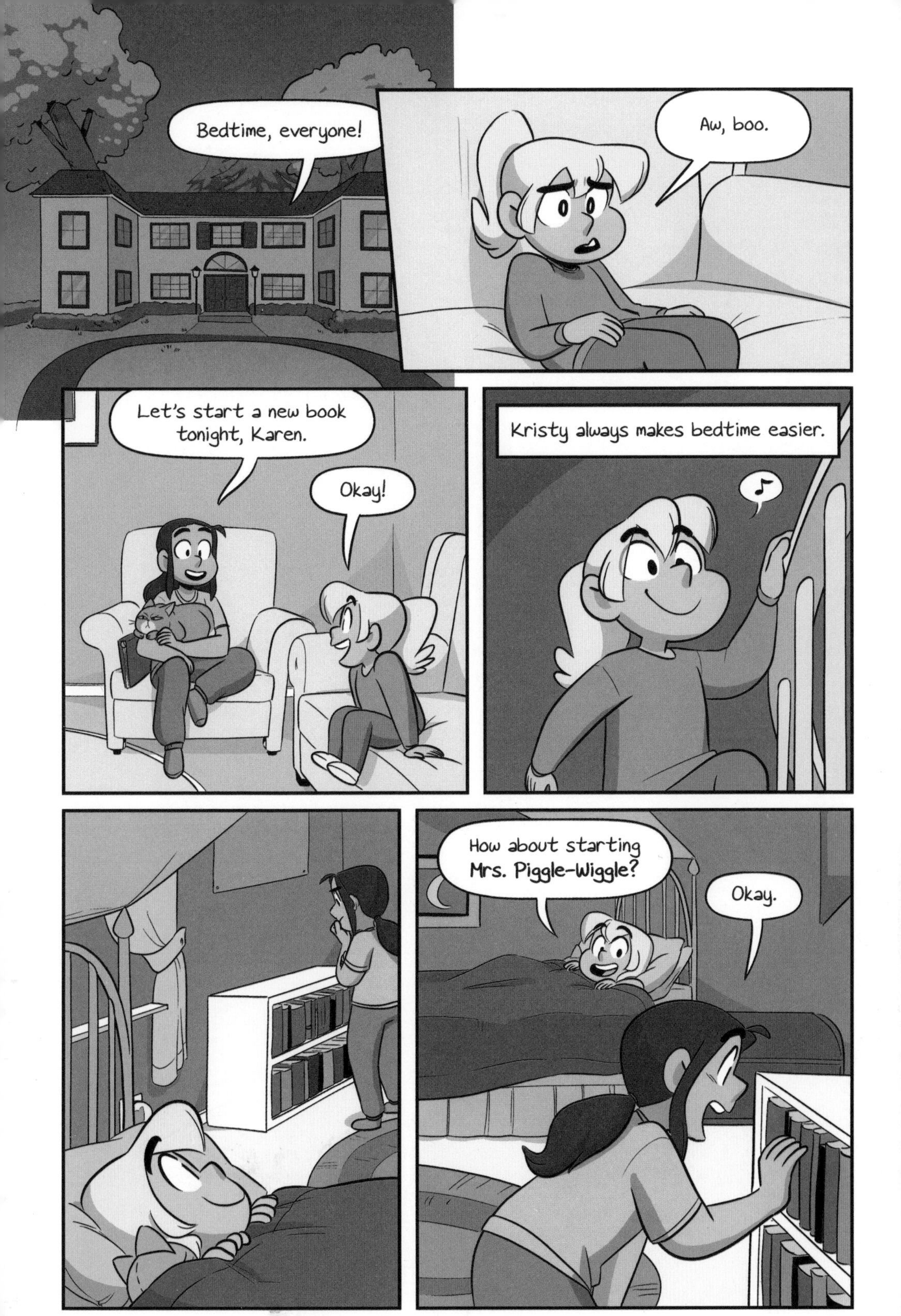
Bedtime, everyone!
Aw, boo.
Let's start a new book tonight, Karen.
Okay!
Kristy always makes bedtime easier.
♪
How about starting **Mrs. Piggle-Wiggle?**
Okay.

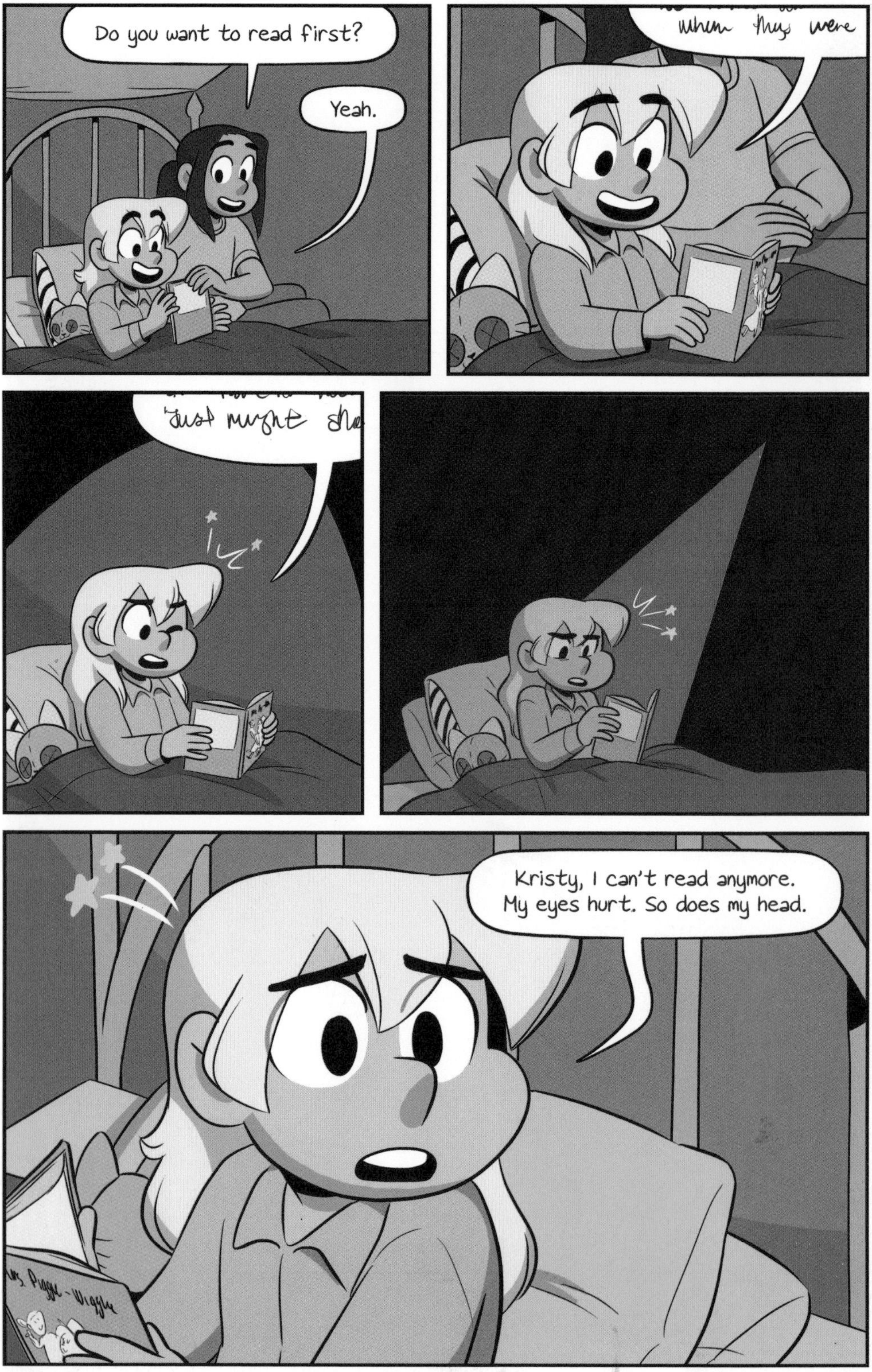
Do you want to read first?
Yeah.
Kristy, I can't read anymore. My eyes hurt. So does my head.

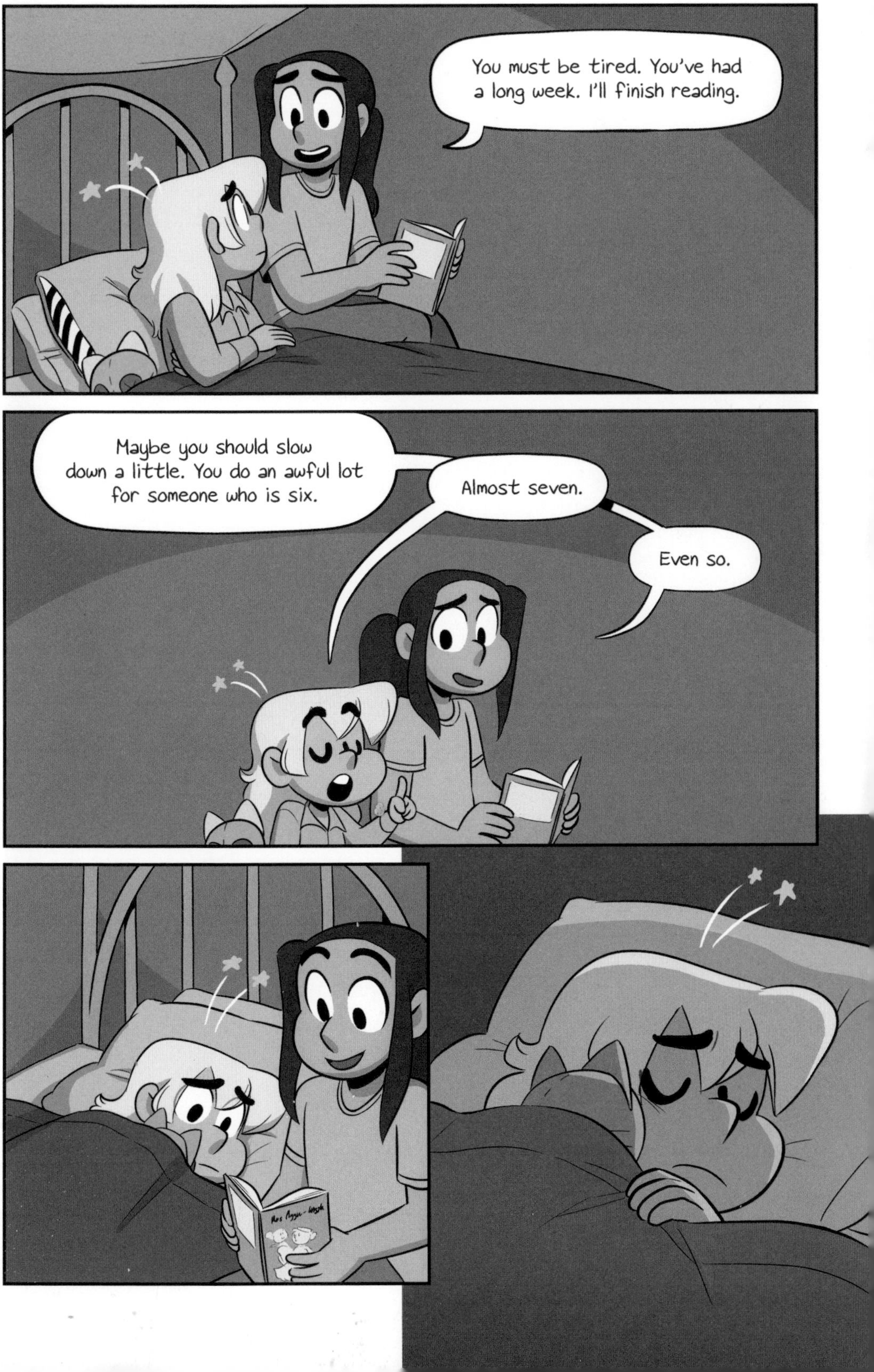
You must be tired. You've had a long week. I'll finish reading.
Maybe you should slow down a little. You do an awful lot for someone who is six.
Almost seven.
Even so.

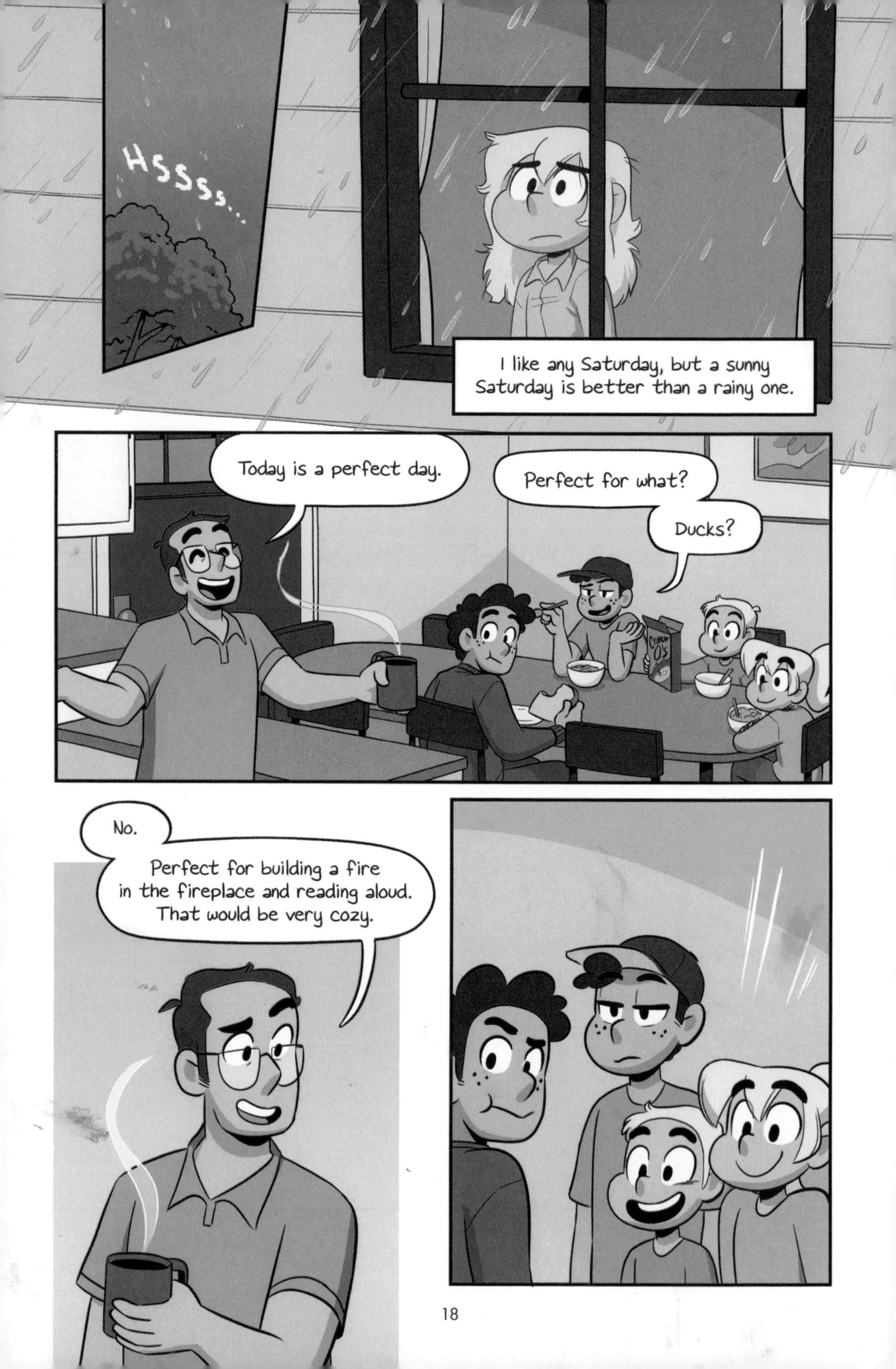
HSSSs...
I like any Saturday, but a sunny Saturday is better than a rainy one.
Today is a perfect day.
Perfect for what?
Ducks?
No.
Perfect for building a fire in the fireplace and reading aloud. That would be very cozy.
Crunch O's

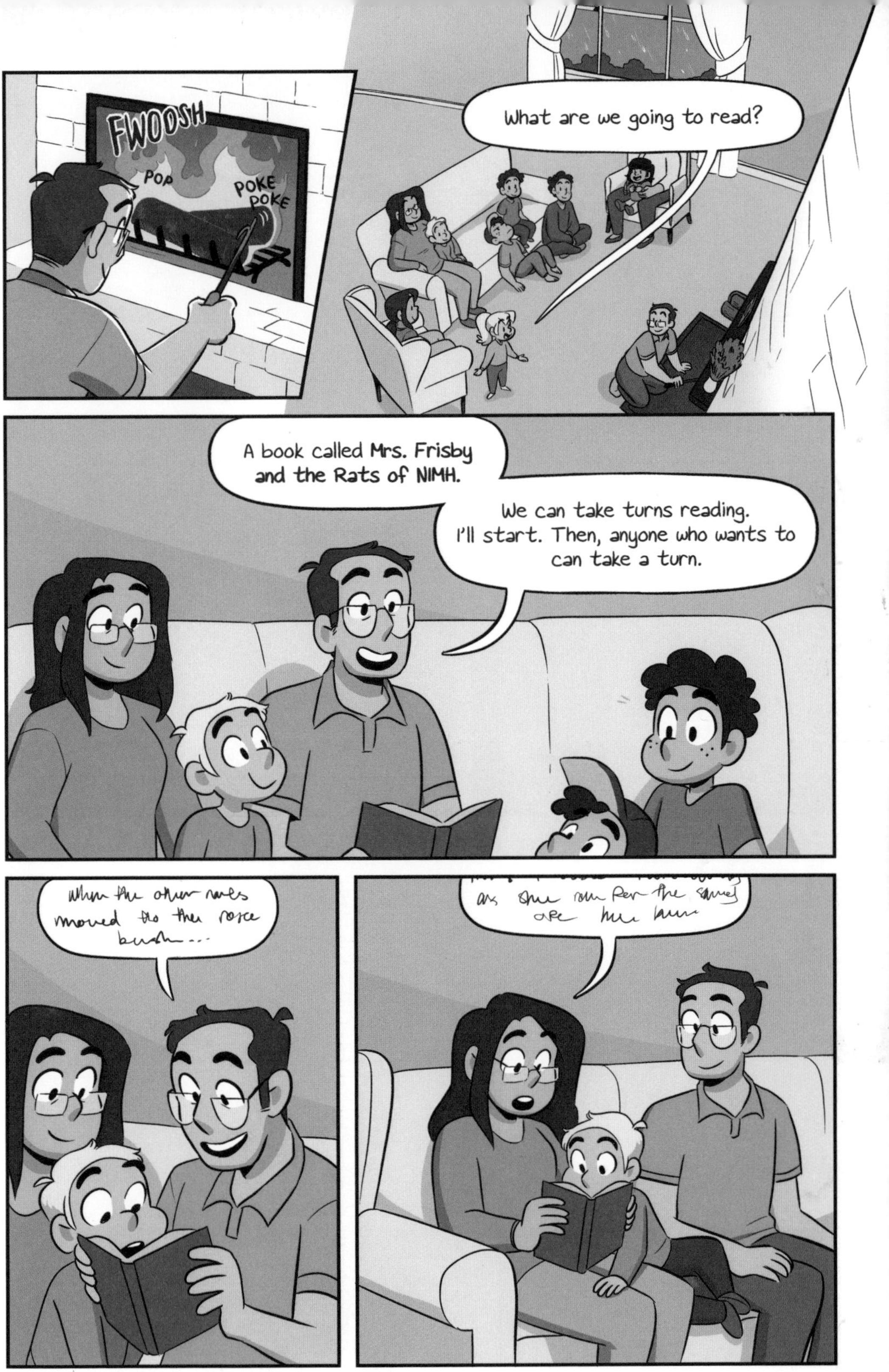
FWOOSH
POP
POKE POKE
What are we going to read?
A book called Mrs. Frisby and the Rats of NIMH.
We can take turns reading. I'll start. Then, anyone who wants to can take a turn.

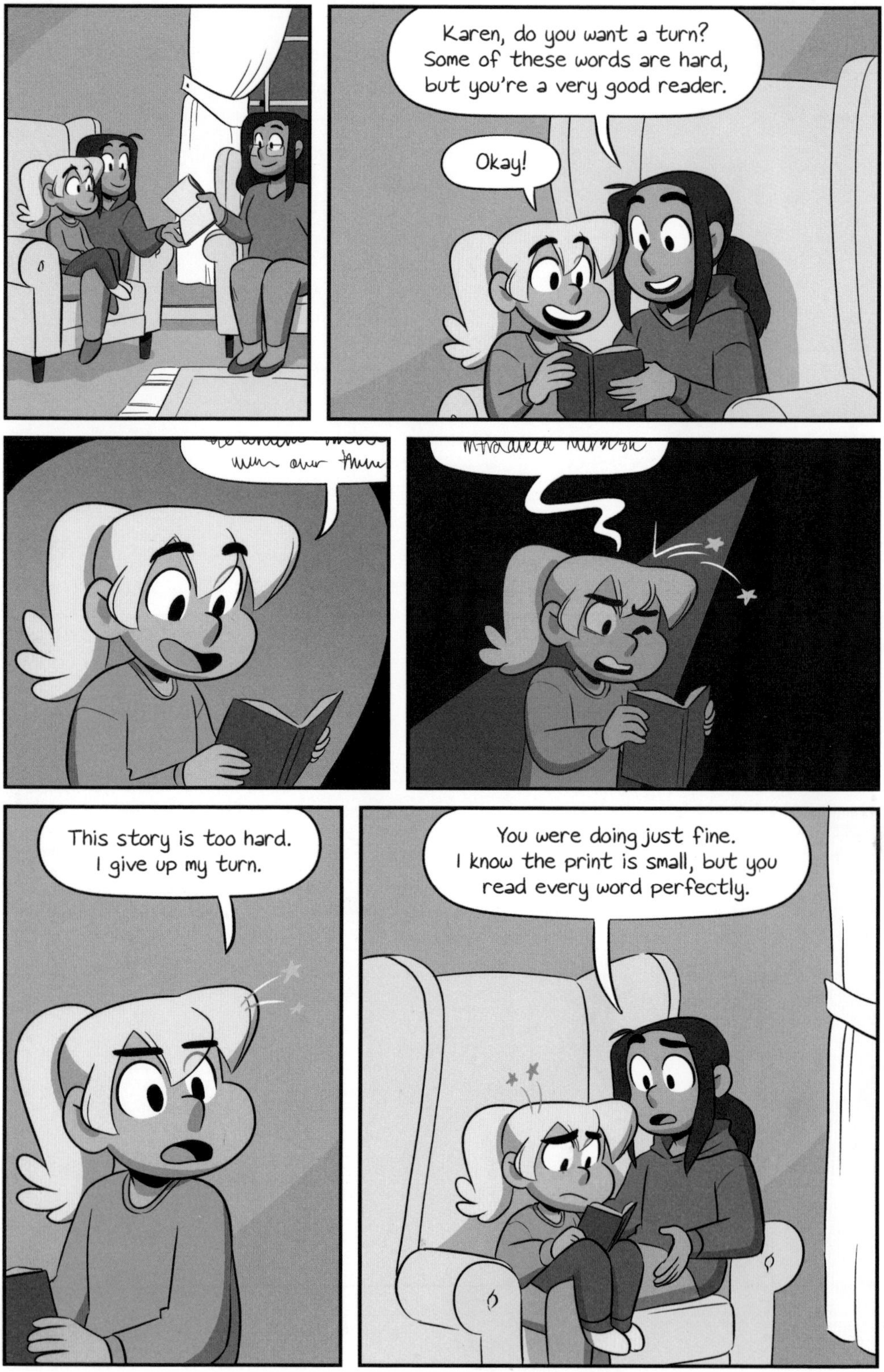
Karen, do you want a turn? Some of these words are hard, but you're a very good reader.
Okay!
This story is too hard. I give up my turn.
You were doing just fine. I know the print is small, but you read every word perfectly.

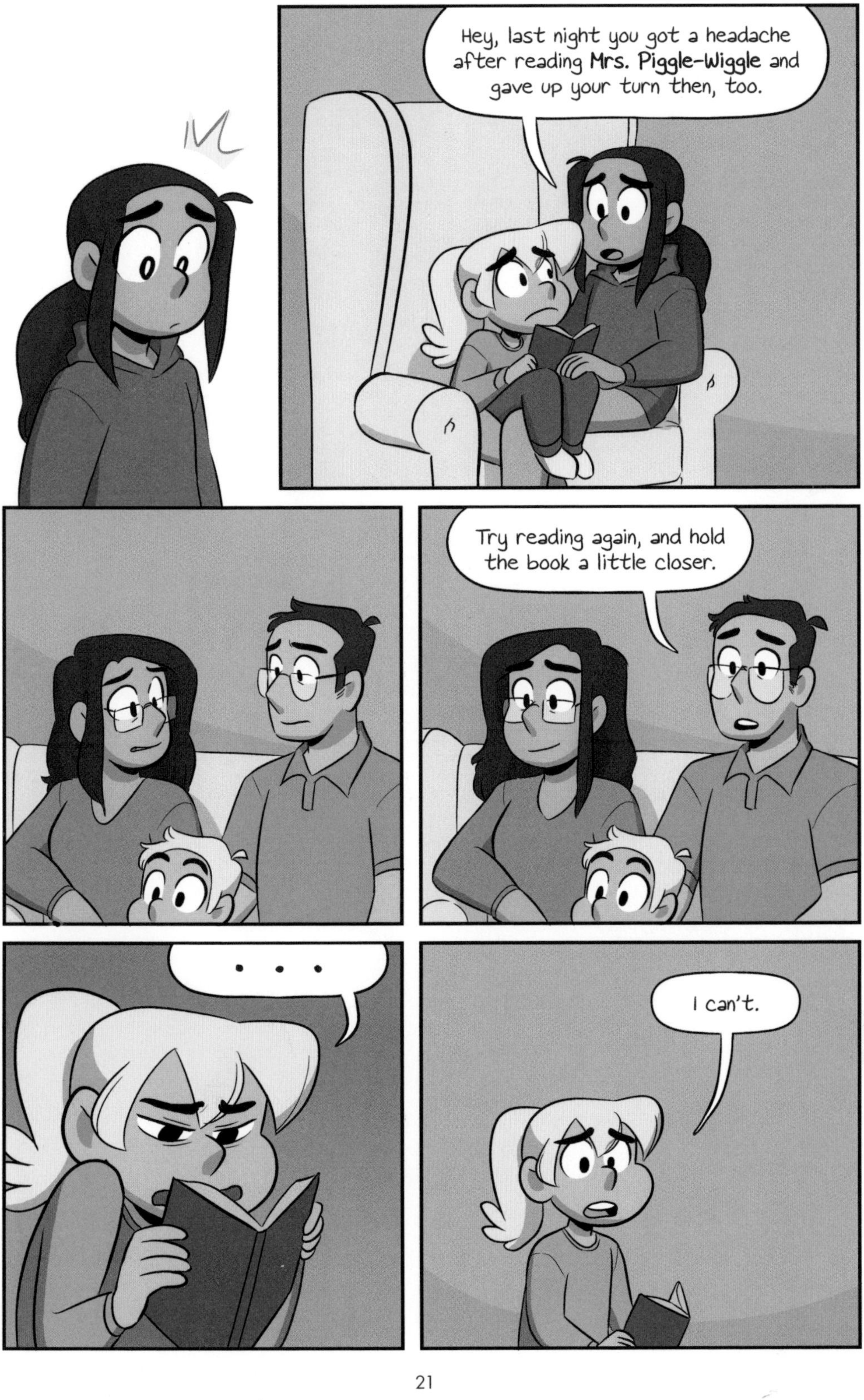

Hey, last night you got a headache after reading **Mrs. Piggle-Wiggle** and gave up your turn then, too.
Try reading again, and hold the book a little closer.
. . .
I can't.

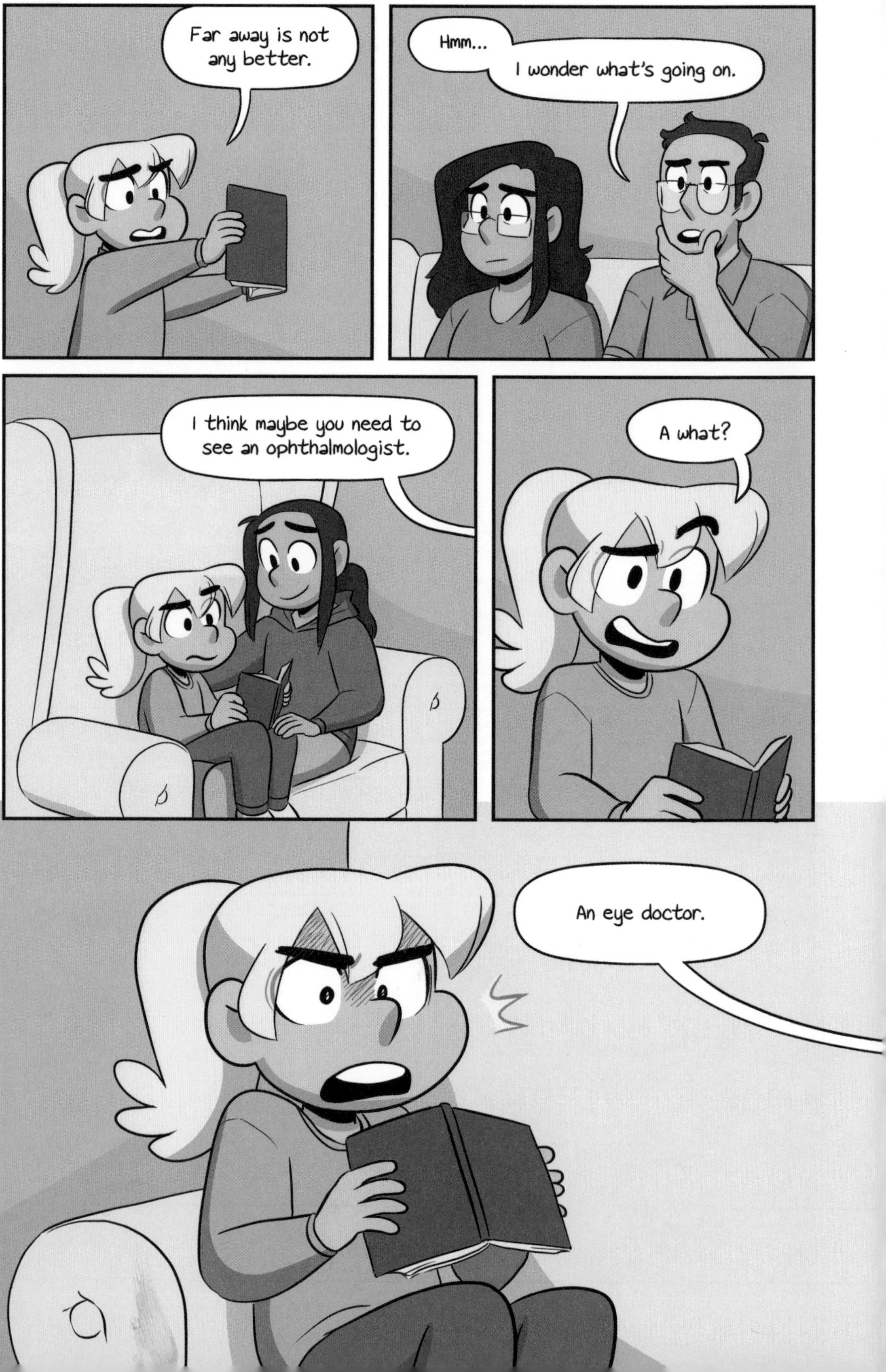
Far away is not any better.
Hmm...
I wonder what's going on.
I think maybe you need to see an ophthalmologist.
A what?
An eye doctor.

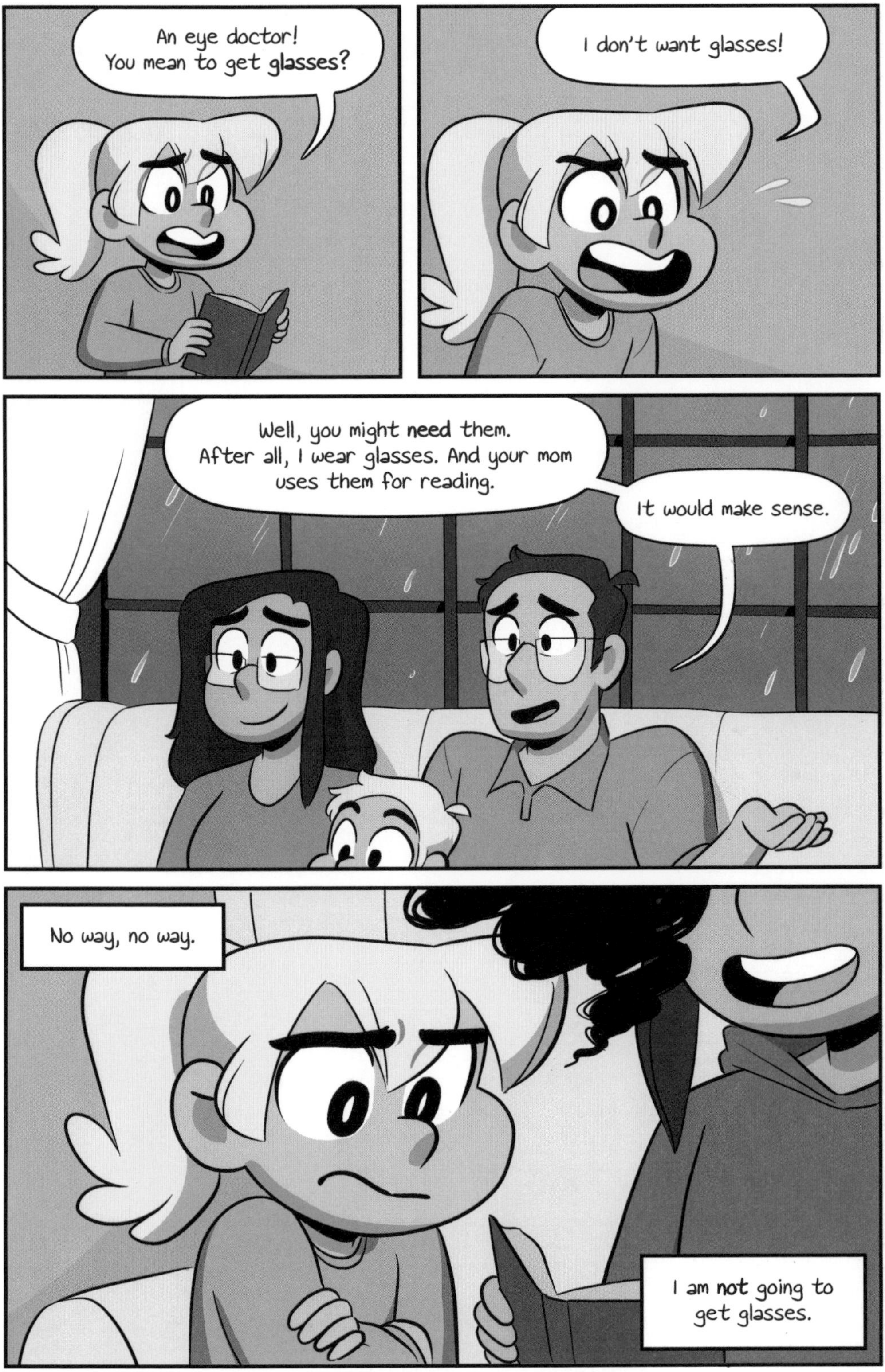
An eye doctor! You mean to get **glasses**?
I don't want glasses!
Well, you might **need** them. After all, I wear glasses. And your mom uses them for reading.
It would make sense.
No way, no way.
I am **not** going to get glasses.

CHAPTER 3

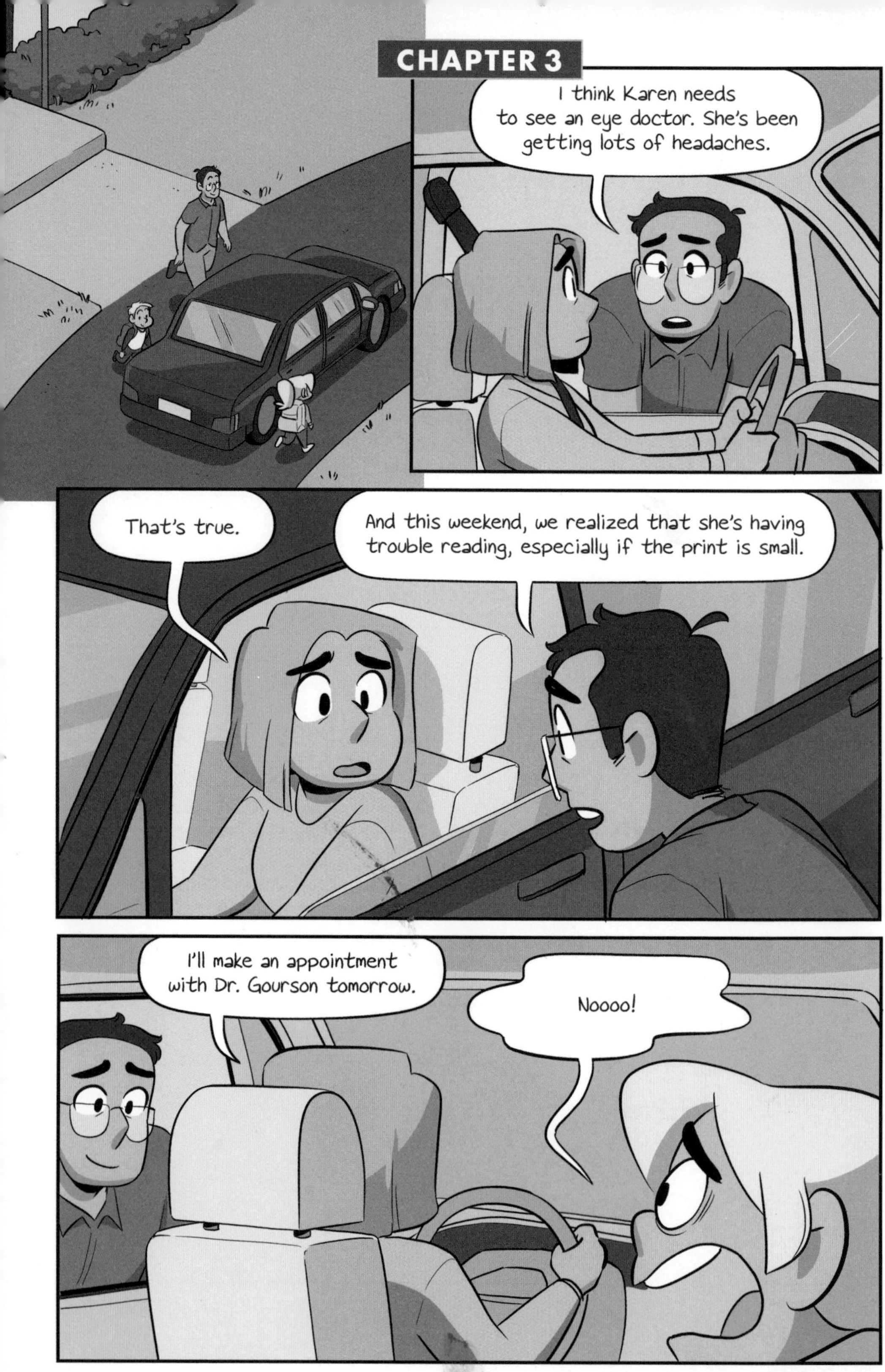

I think Karen needs to see an eye doctor. She's been getting lots of headaches.
That's true.
And this weekend, we realized that she's having trouble reading, especially if the print is small.
I'll make an appointment with Dr. Gourson tomorrow.
Noooo!

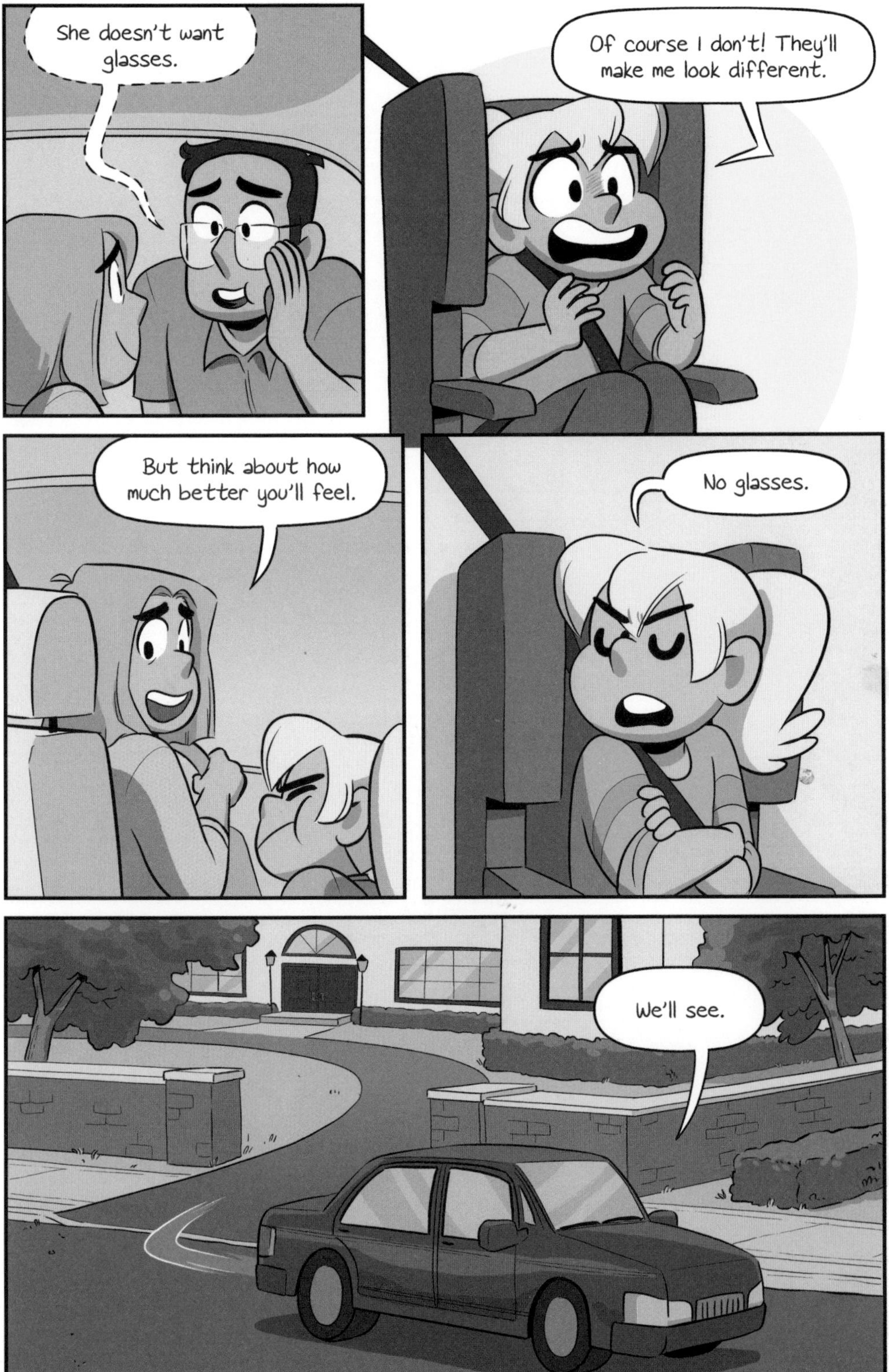
She doesn't want glasses.
Of course I don't! They'll make me look different.
But think about how much better you'll feel.
No glasses.
We'll see.

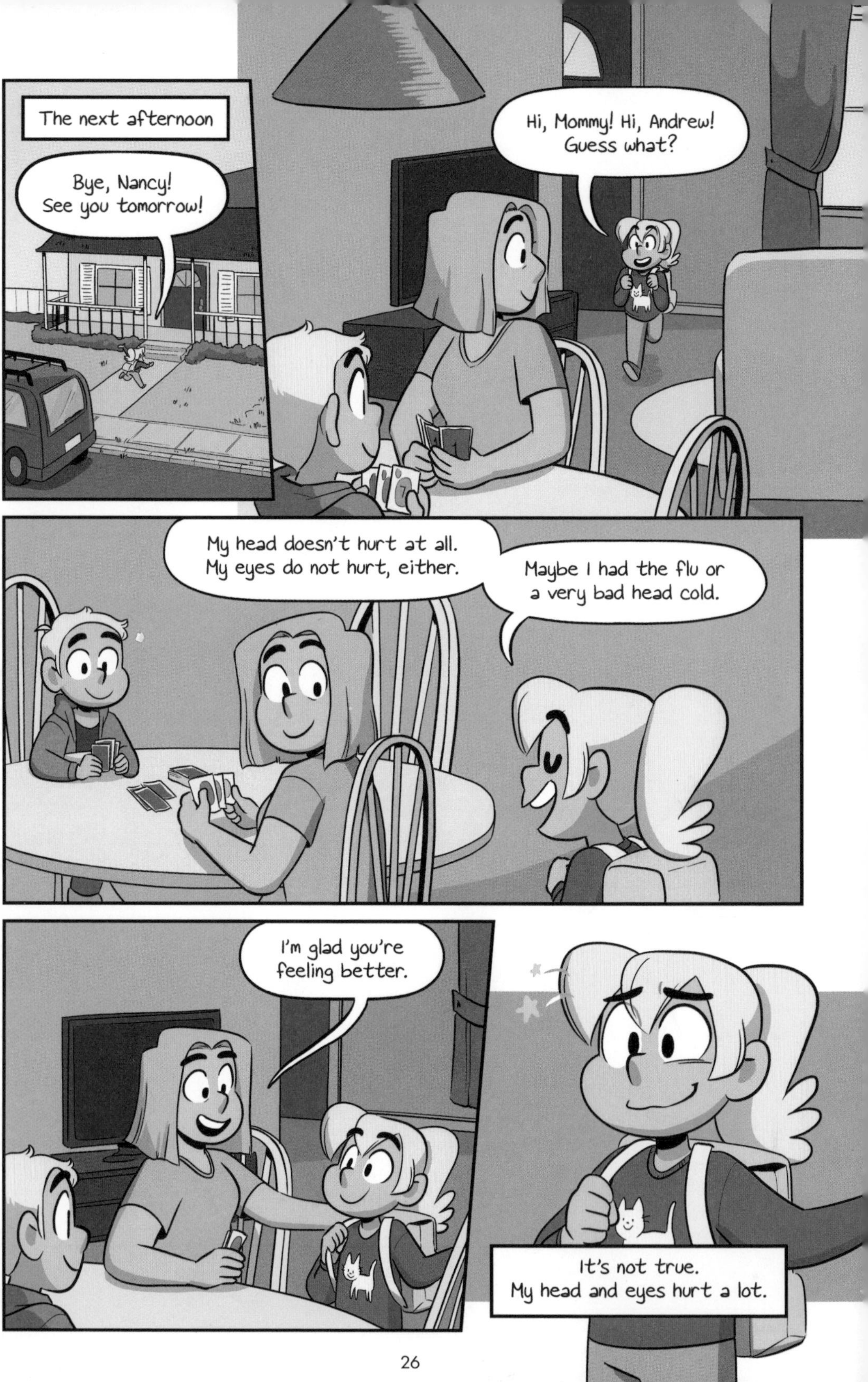
The next afternoon
Bye, Nancy! See you tomorrow!
Hi, Mommy! Hi, Andrew! Guess what?
My head doesn't hurt at all. My eyes do not hurt, either.
Maybe I had the flu or a very bad head cold.
I'm glad you're feeling better.
It's not true. My head and eyes hurt a lot.

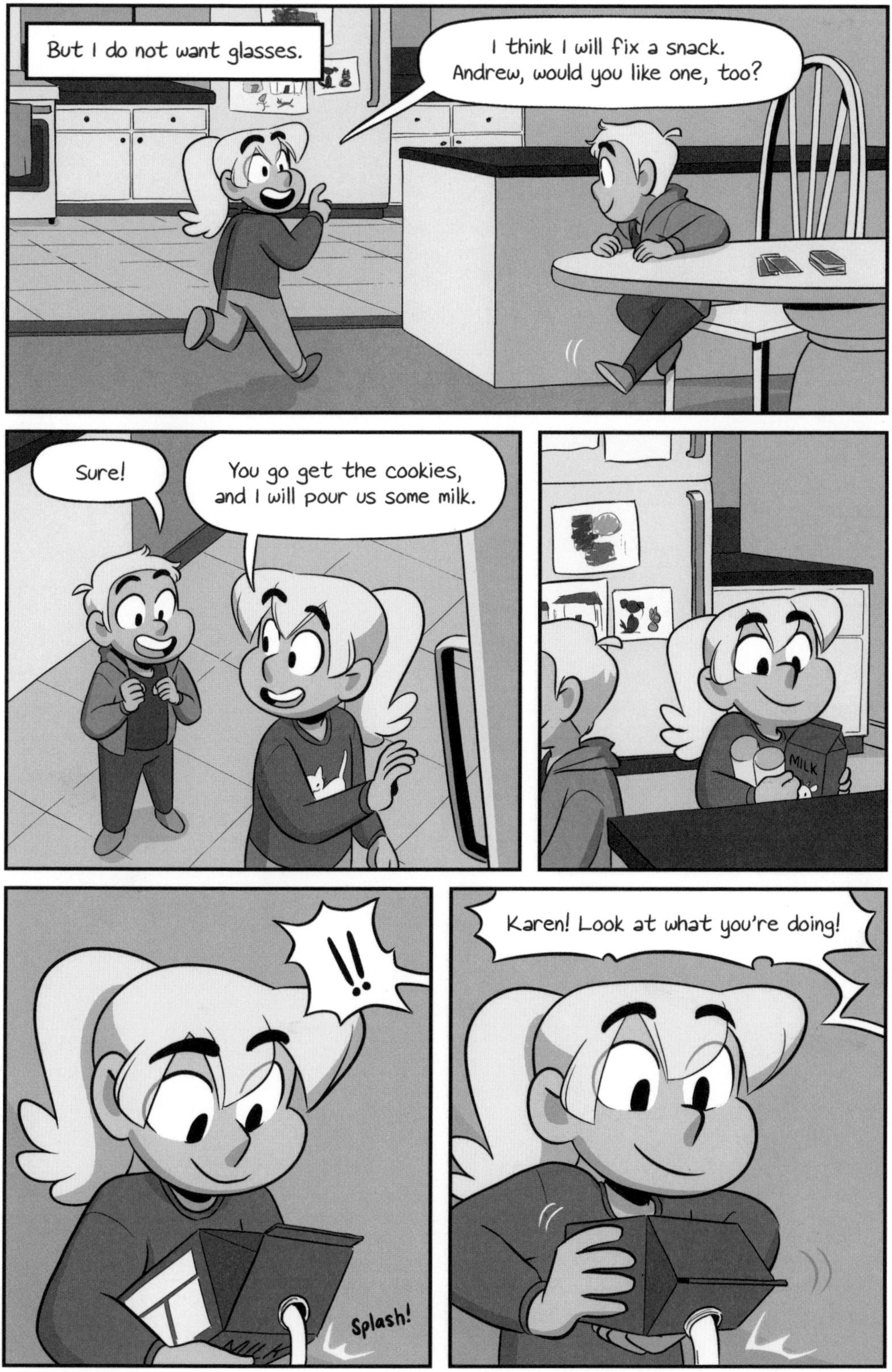

But I do not want glasses.
I think I will fix a snack. Andrew, would you like one, too?
Sure!
You go get the cookies, and I will pour us some milk.
MILK
!!
Splash!
Karen! Look at what you're doing!

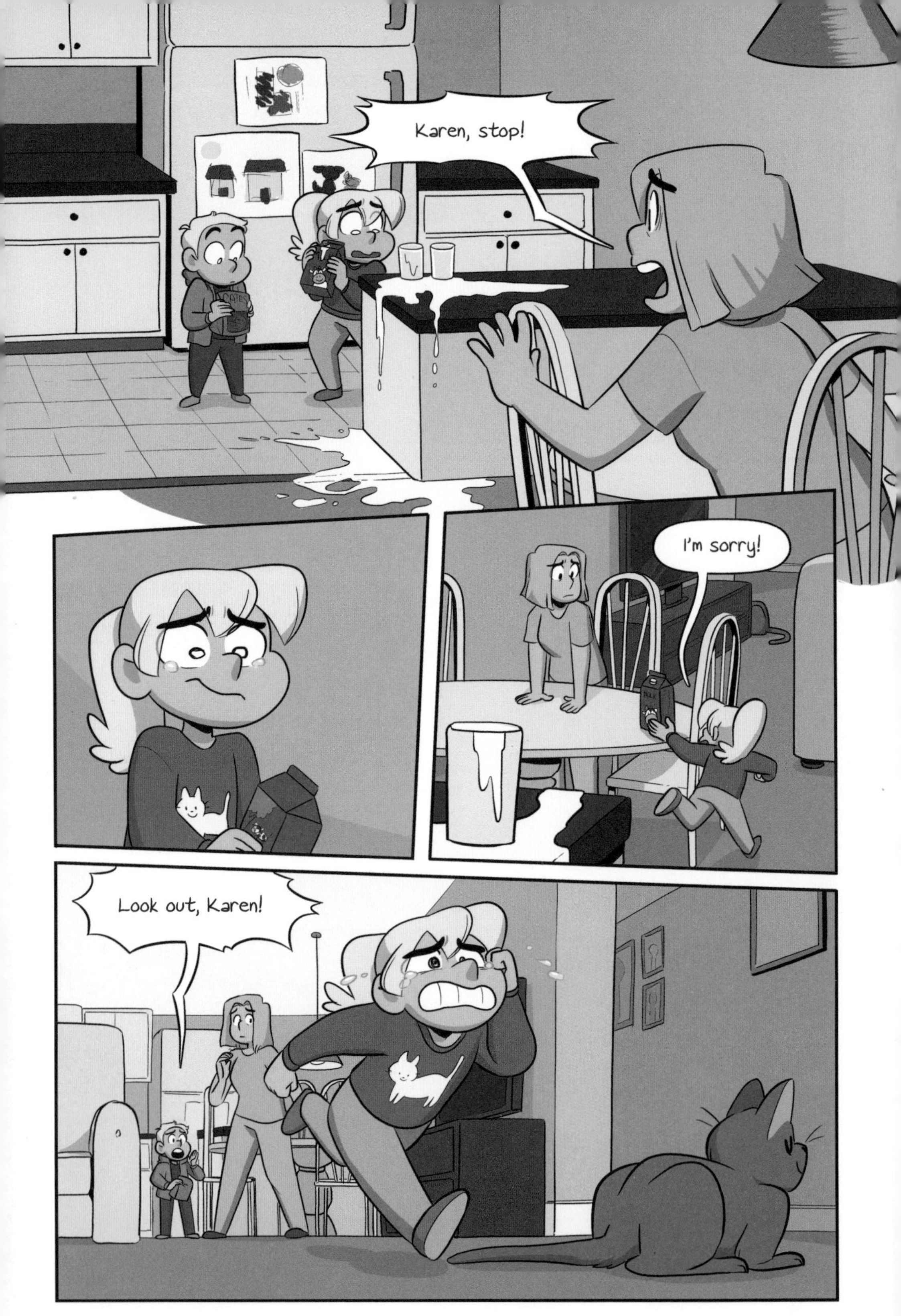
Karen, stop!
I'm sorry!
Look out, Karen!

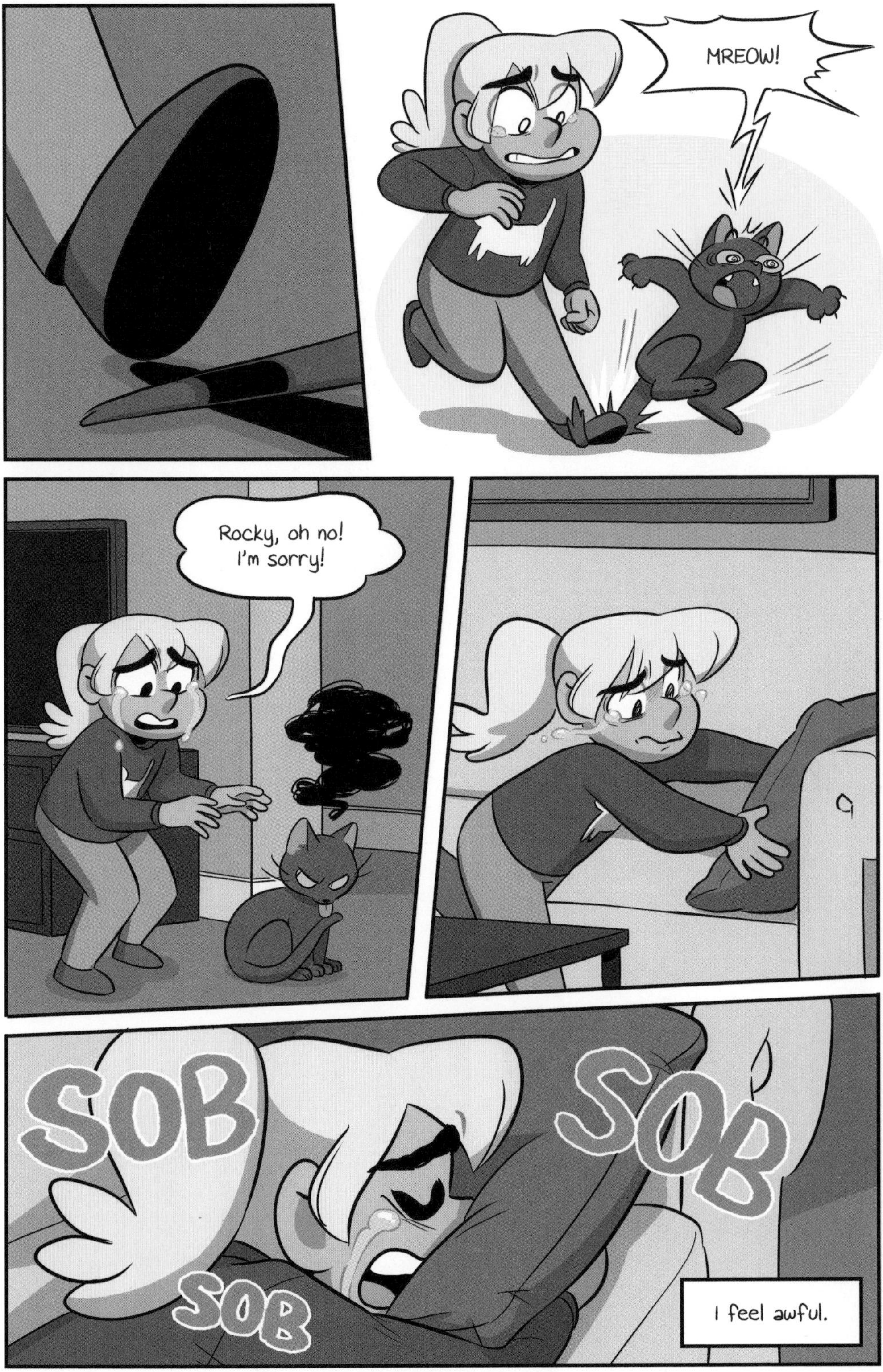
MREOW!
Rocky, oh no! I'm sorry!
SOB
SOB
SOB
I feel awful.

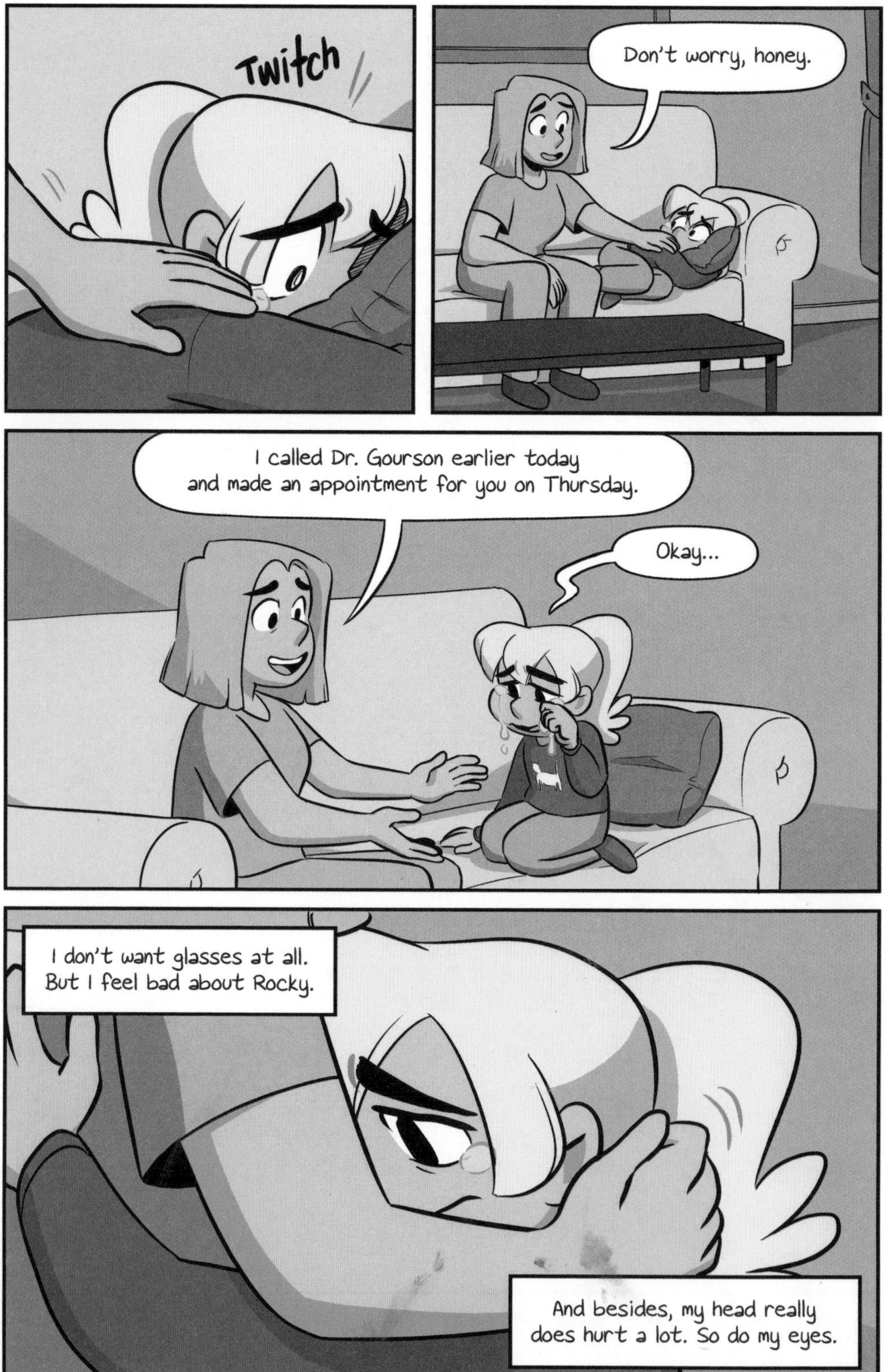
Twitch
Don't worry, honey.
I called Dr. Gourson earlier today and made an appointment for you on Thursday.
Okay...
I don't want glasses at all. But I feel bad about Rocky.
And besides, my head really does hurt a lot. So do my eyes.

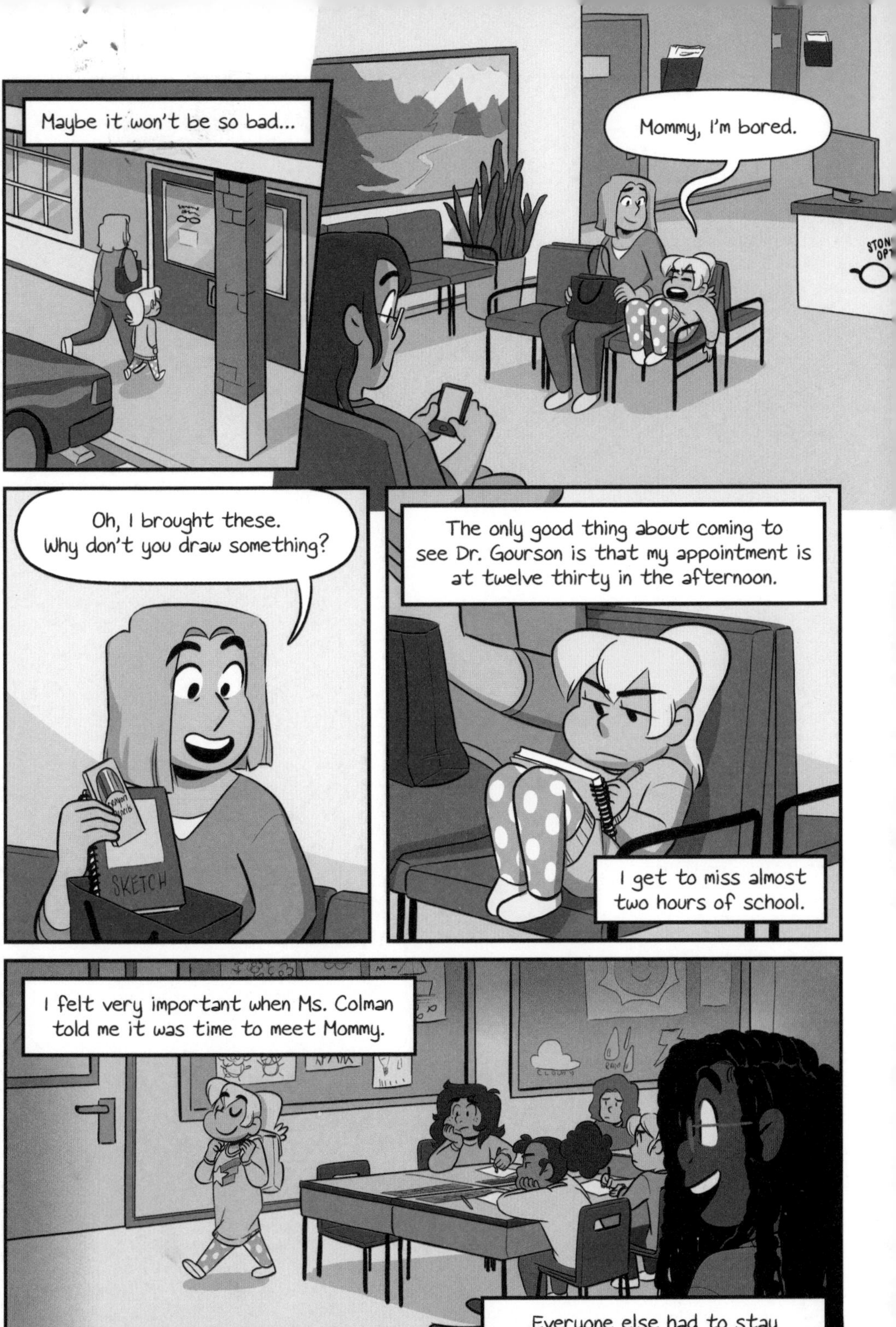

Maybe it won't be so bad...
Mommy, I'm bored.
Oh, I brought these.
Why don't you draw something?
SKETCH
The only good thing about coming to see Dr. Gourson is that my appointment is at twelve thirty in the afternoon.
I get to miss almost two hours of school.
I felt very important when Ms. Colman told me it was time to meet Mommy.
Everyone else had to stay and work on subtraction problems.

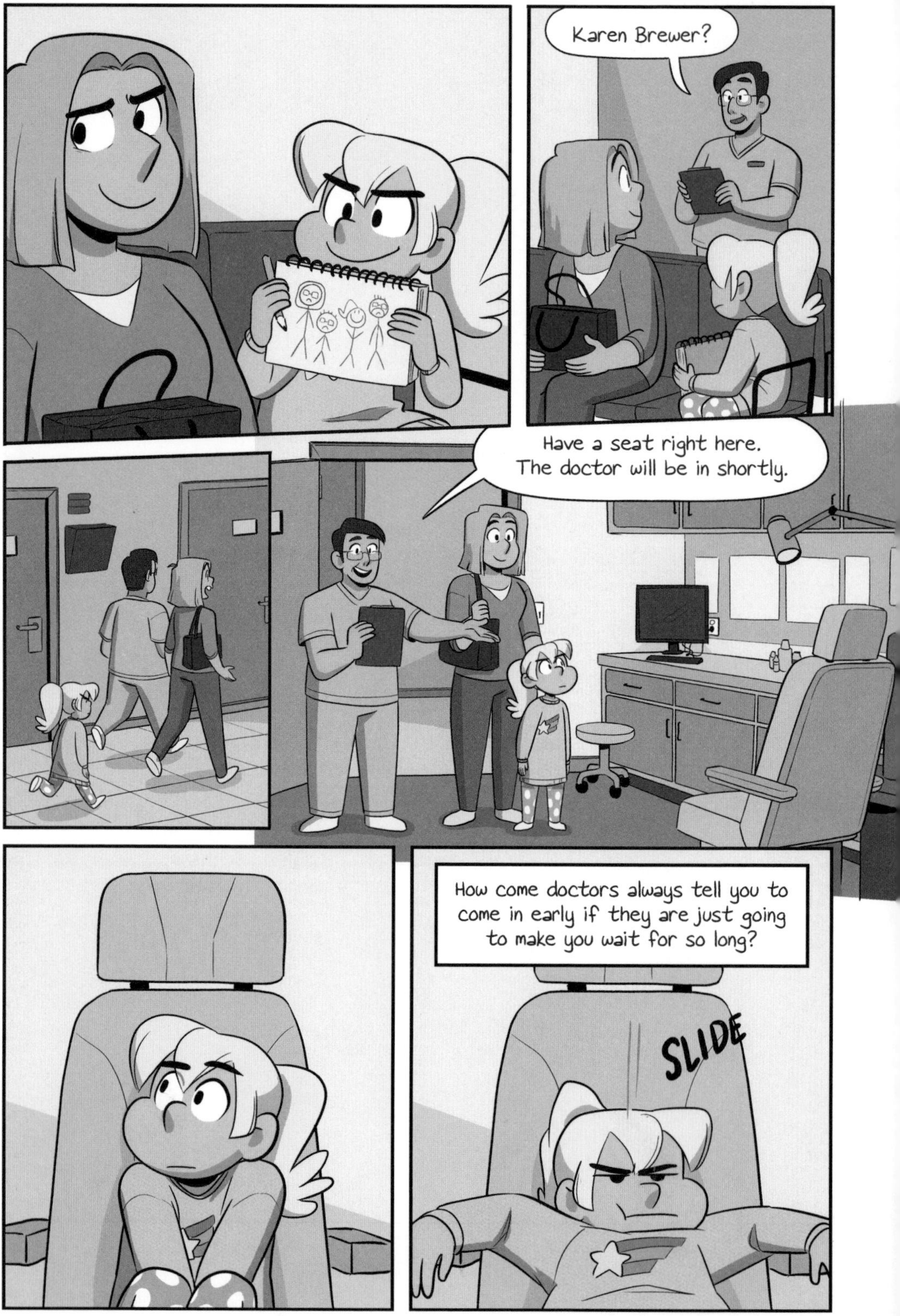
Karen Brewer?
Have a seat right here. The doctor will be in shortly.
How come doctors always tell you to come in early if they are just going to make you wait for so long?
SLIDE

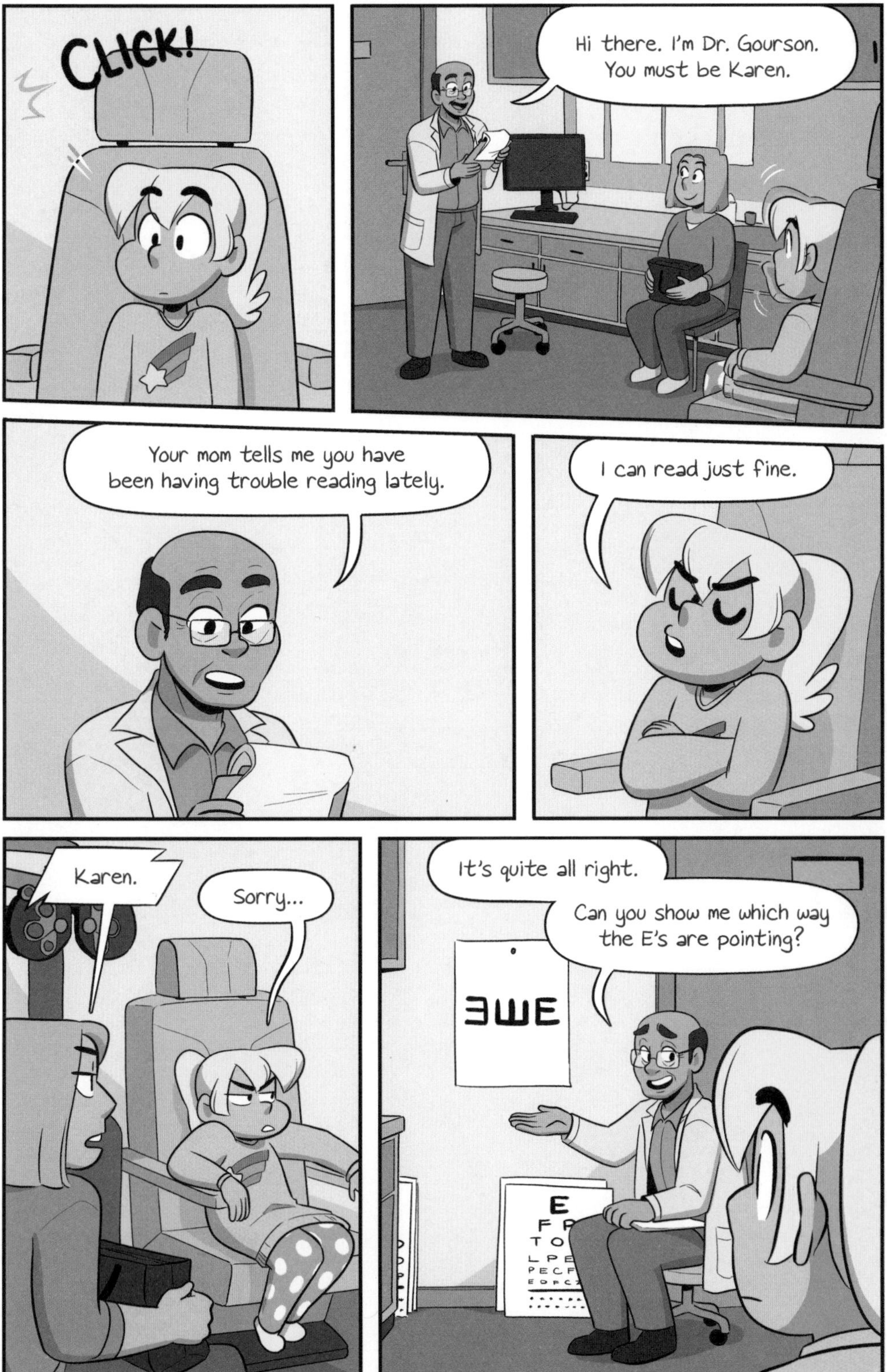
CLICK!
Hi there. I'm Dr. Gourson.
You must be Karen.
Your mom tells me you have been having trouble reading lately.
I can read just fine.
Karen.
Sorry...
It's quite all right.
Can you show me which way the E's are pointing?
E

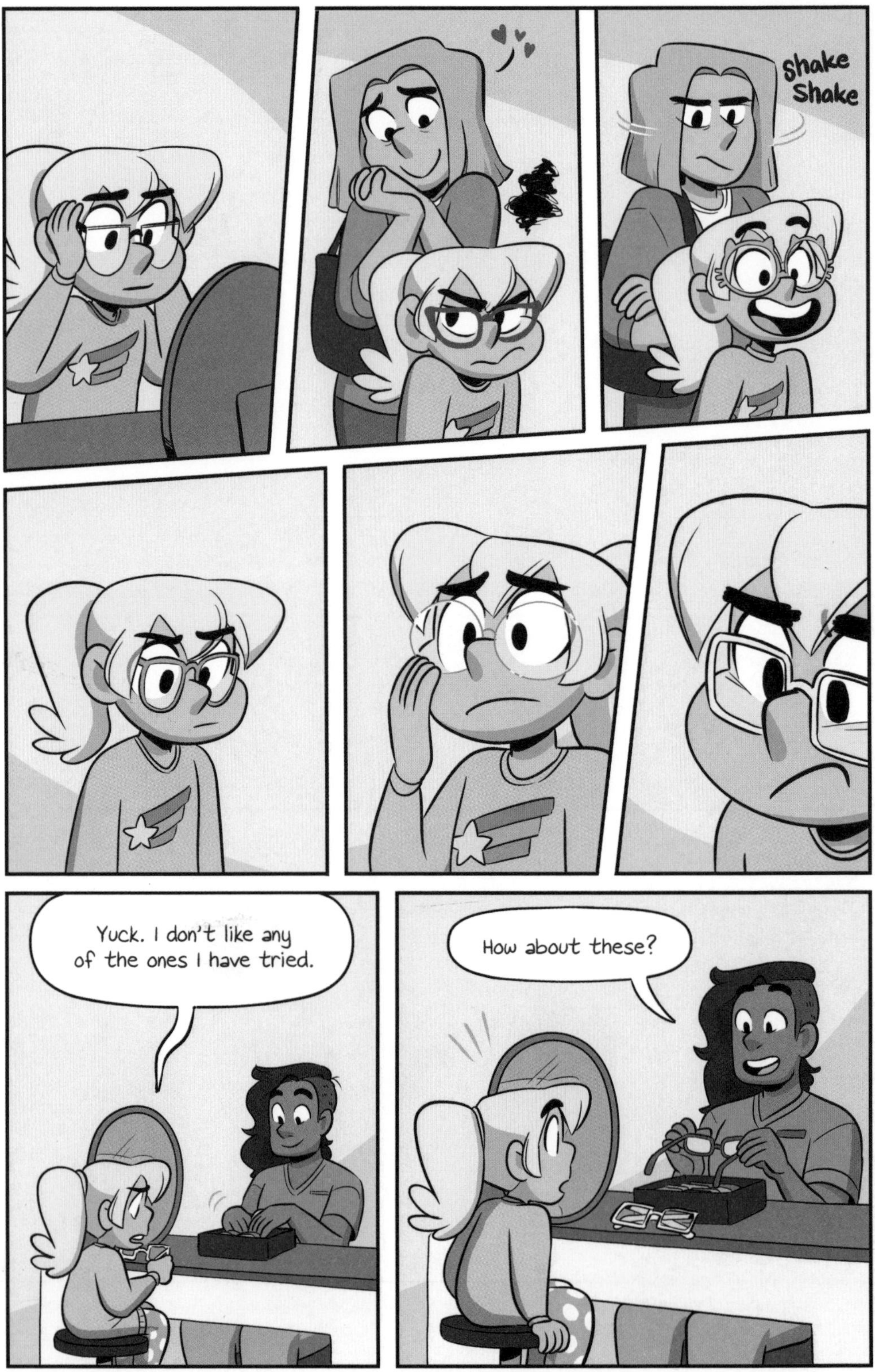
Shake
Shake
Yuck. I don't like any of the ones I have tried.
How about these?

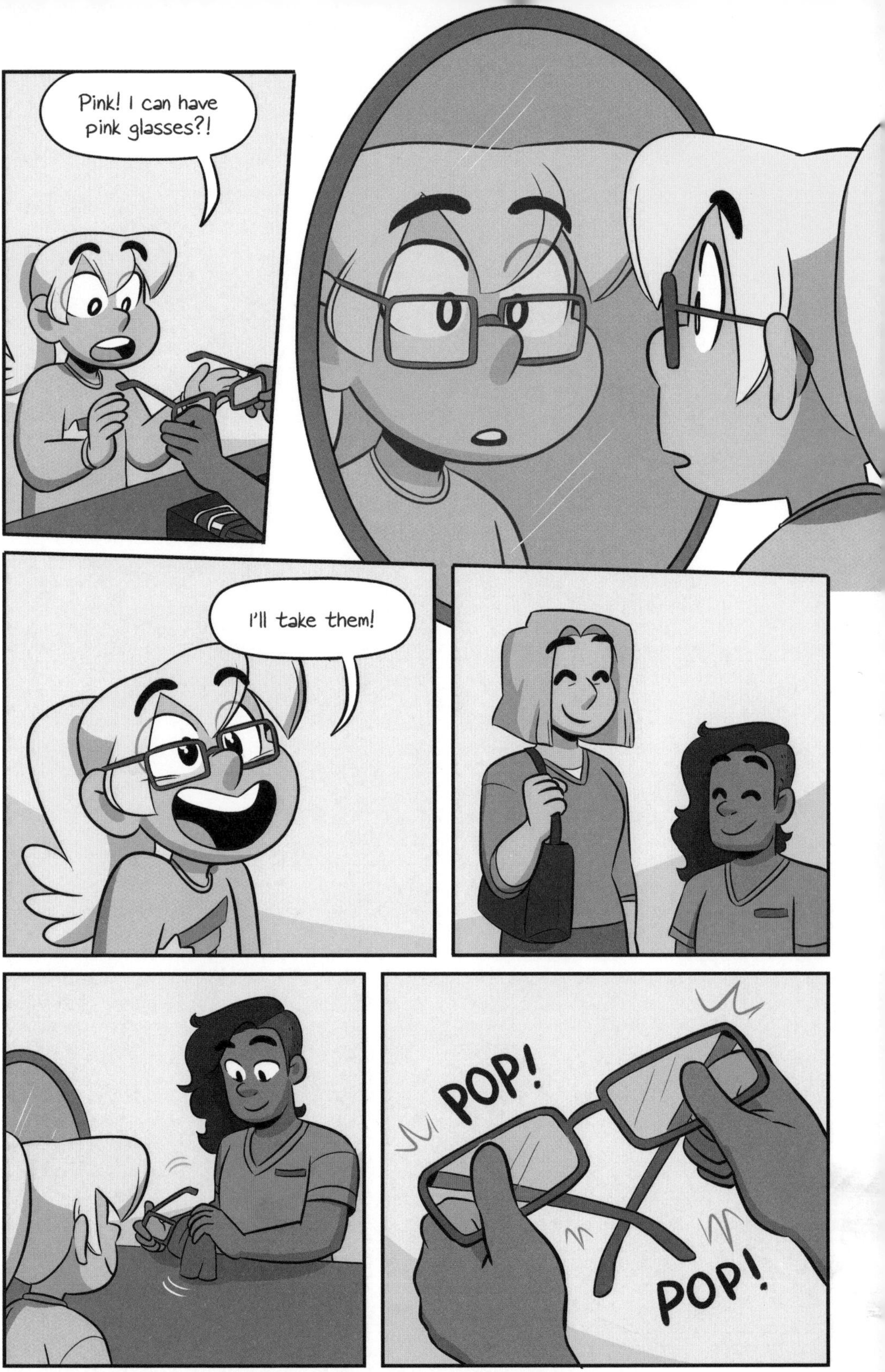
Pink! I can have pink glasses?!
I'll take them!
POP!
POP!

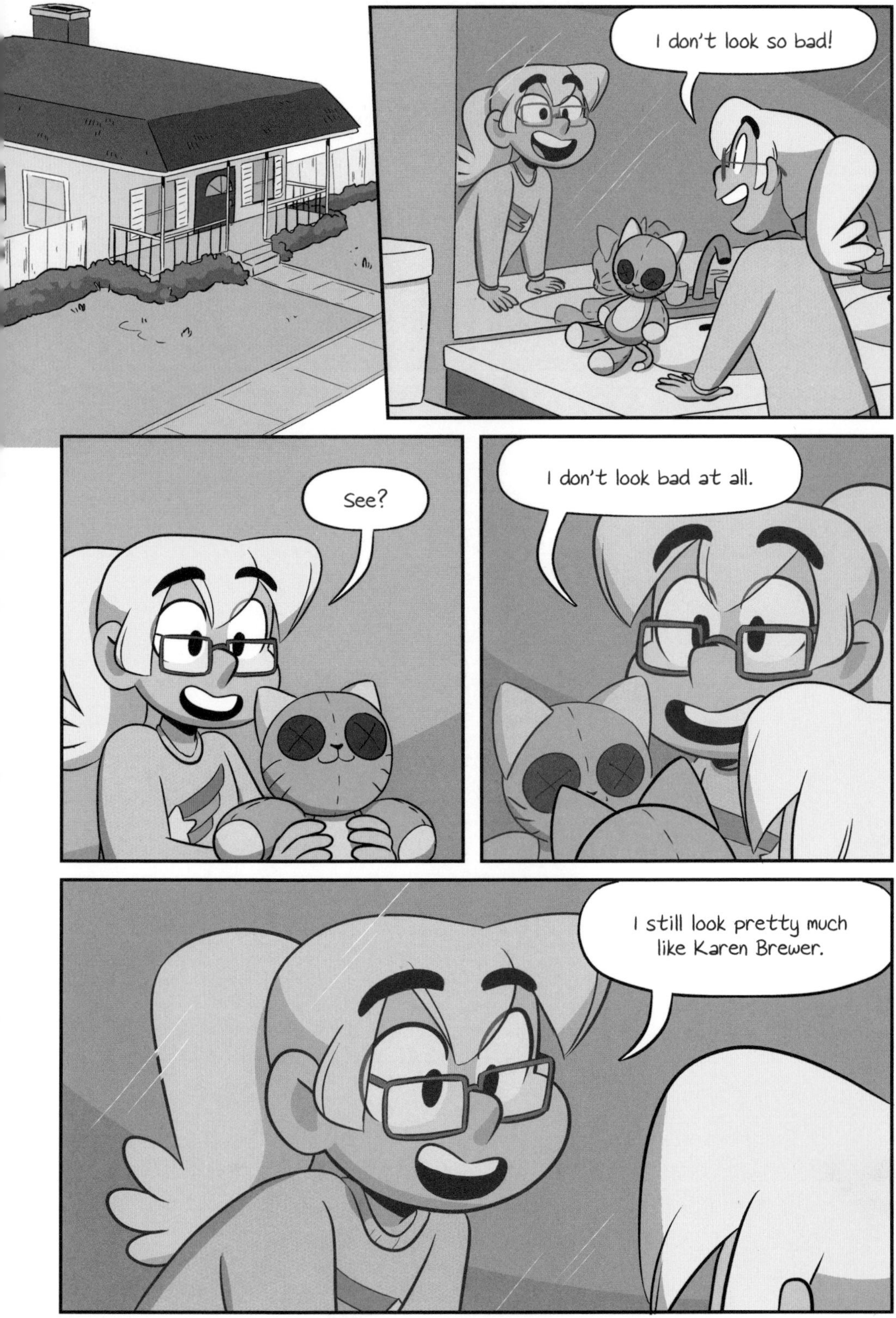
I don't look so bad!
See?
I don't look bad at all.
I still look pretty much like Karen Brewer.

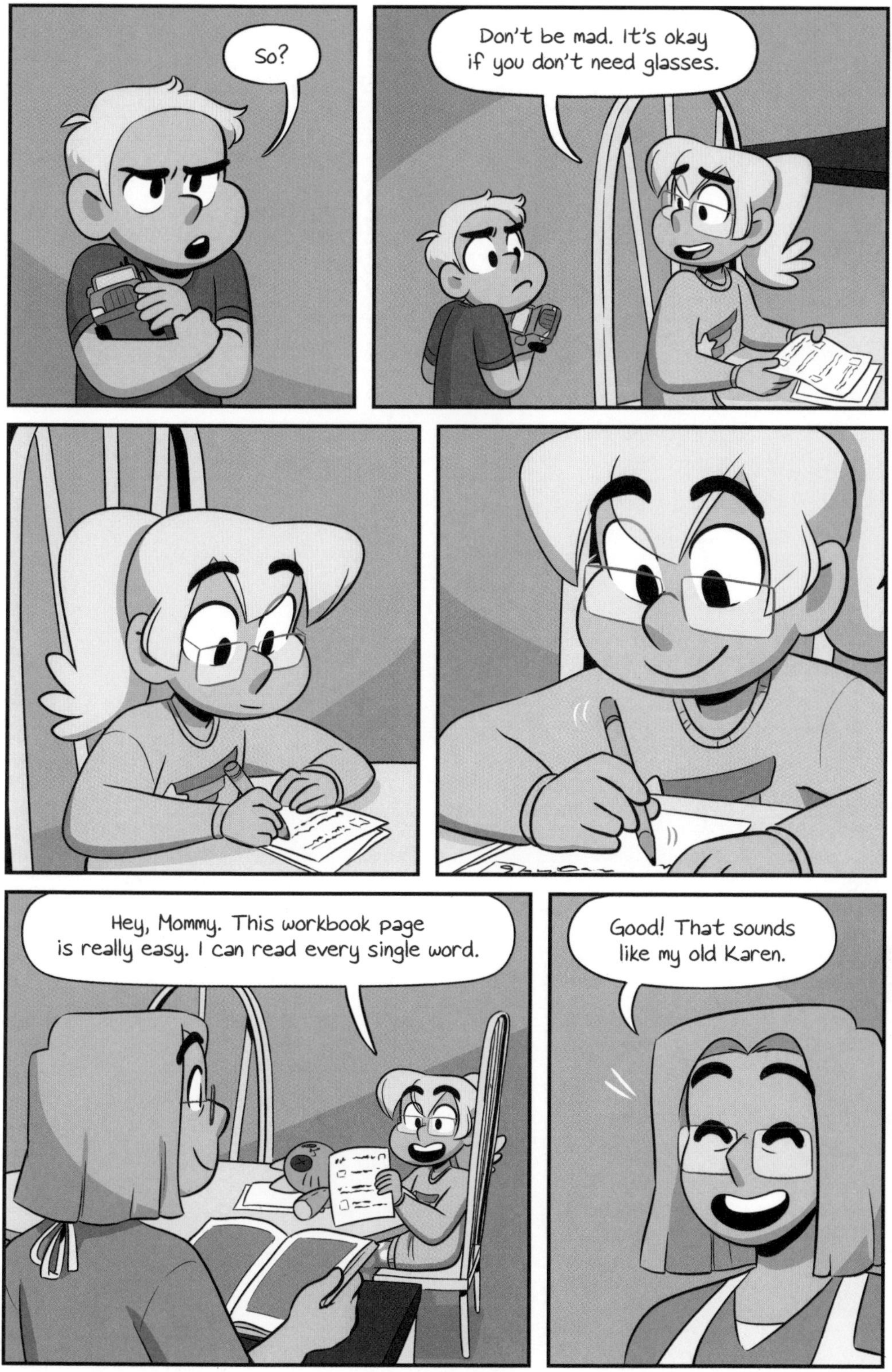
So?
Don't be mad. It's okay if you don't need glasses.
Hey, Mommy. This workbook page is really easy. I can read every single word.
Good! That sounds like my old Karen.

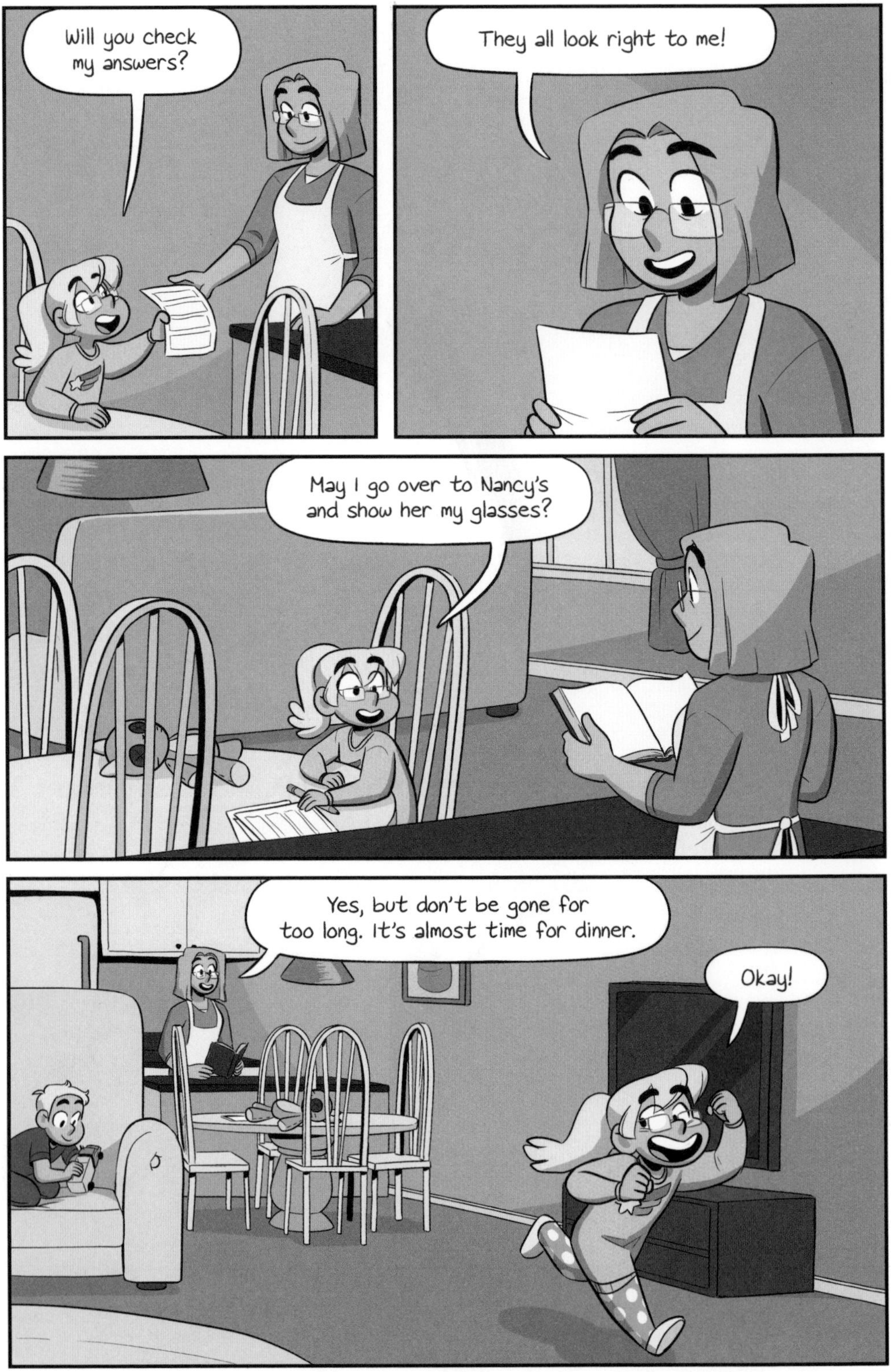
Will you check my answers?
They all look right to me!
May I go over to Nancy's and show her my glasses?
Yes, but don't be gone for too long. It's almost time for dinner.
Okay!

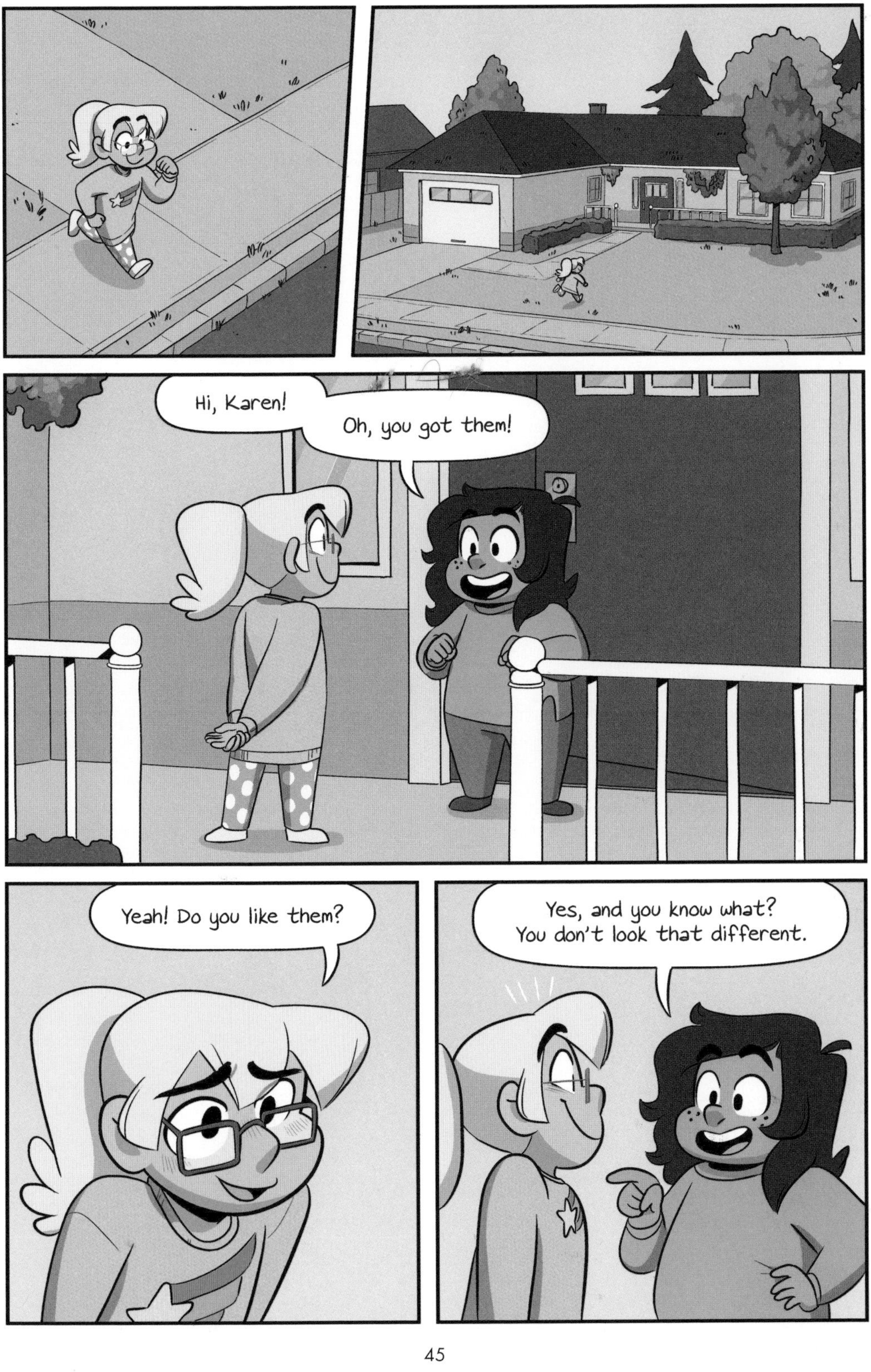
Hi, Karen!
Oh, you got them!
Yeah! Do you like them?
Yes, and you know what?
You don't look that different.

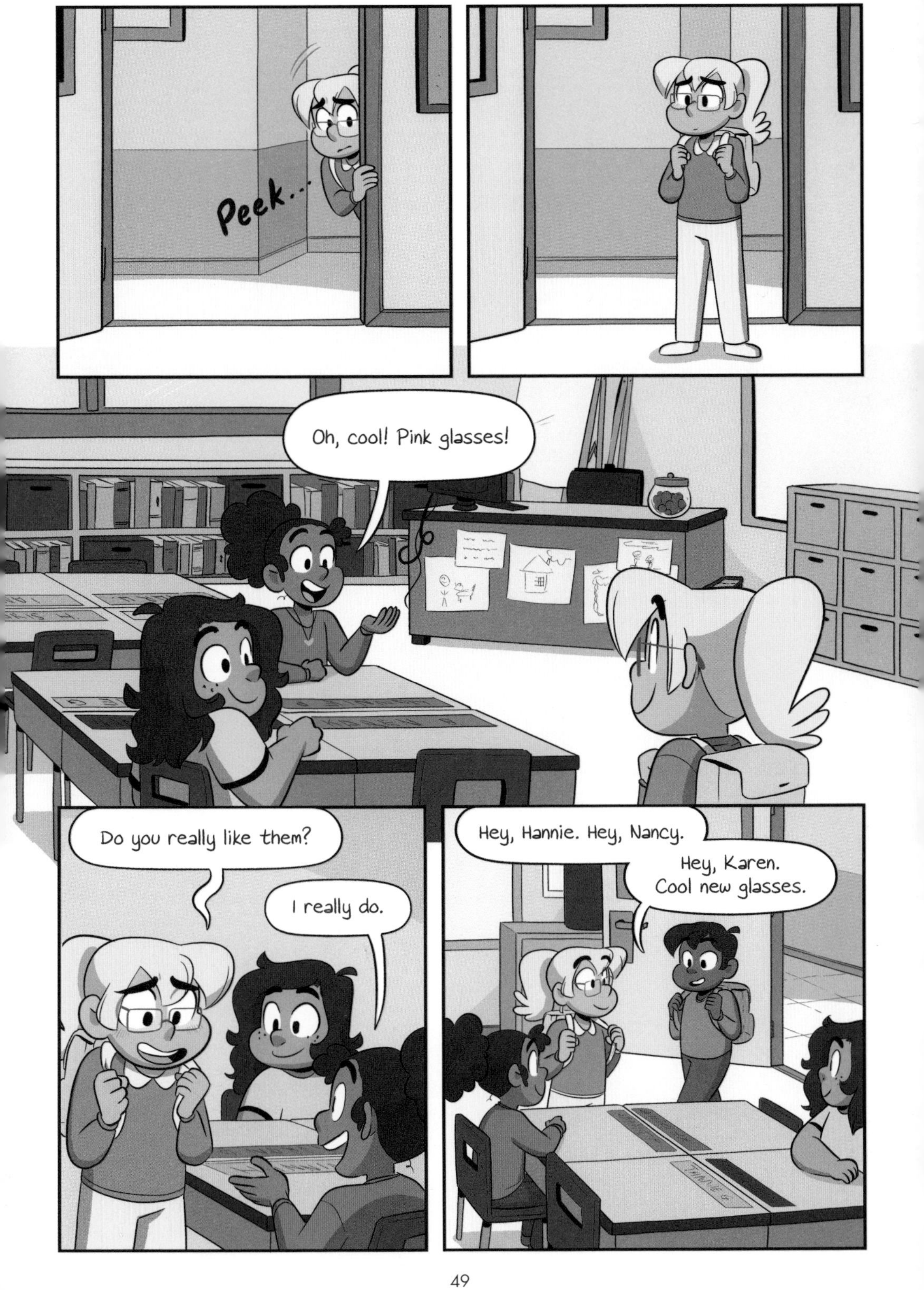
Peek...
Oh, cool! Pink glasses!
Do you really like them?
I really do.
Hey, Hannie. Hey, Nancy.
Hey, Karen.
Cool new glasses.

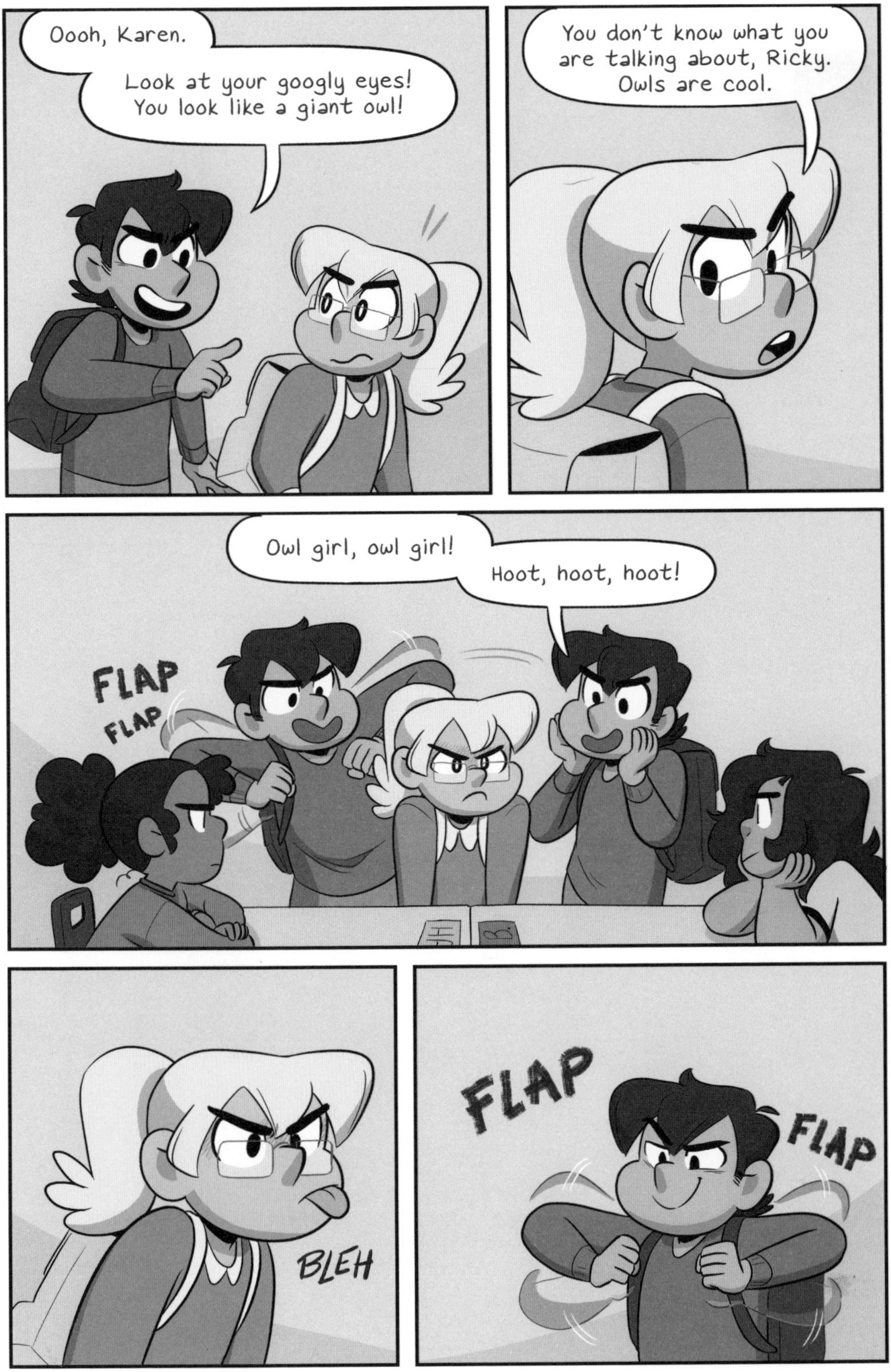

Oooh, Karen.
Look at your googly eyes! You look like a giant owl!
You don't know what you are talking about, Ricky. Owls are cool.
Owl girl, owl girl!
Hoot, hoot, hoot!
FLAP
FLAP
BLEH
FLAP
FLAP

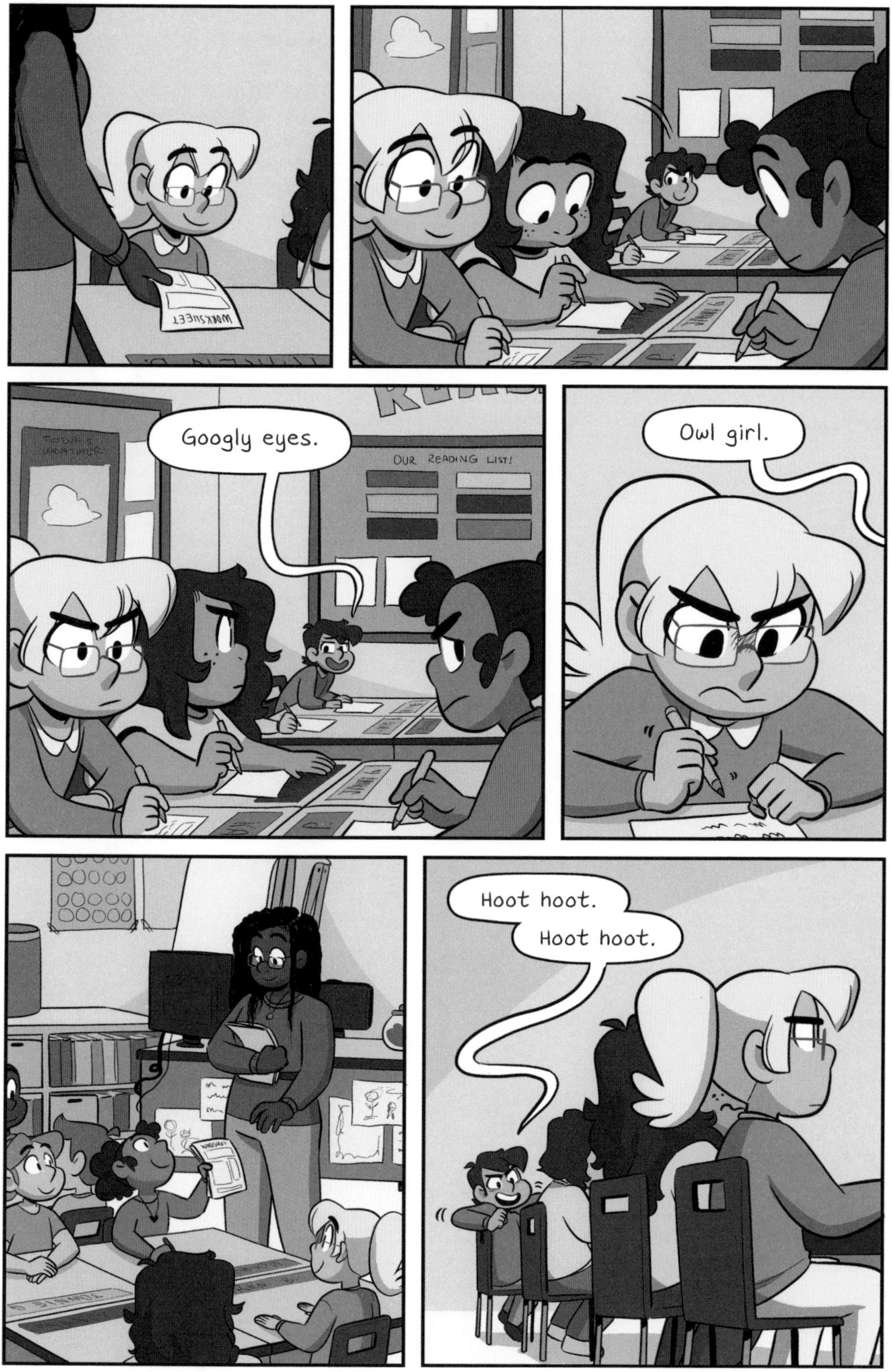
OUR READING LIST!
Googly eyes.
Owl girl.
Hoot hoot.
Hoot hoot.

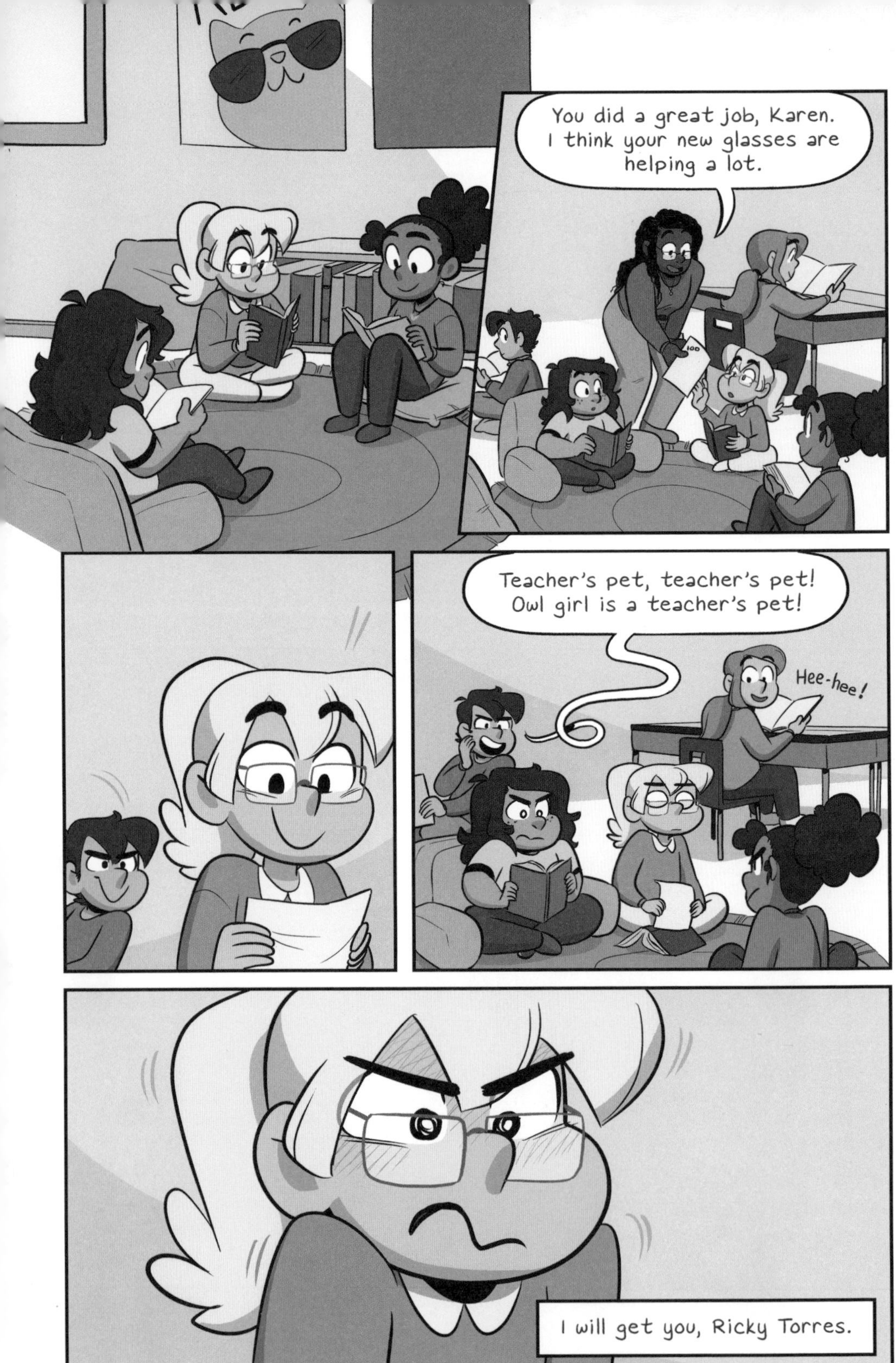
You did a great job, Karen. I think your new glasses are helping a lot.
Teacher's pet, teacher's pet! Owl girl is a teacher's pet!
Hee-hee!
I will get you, Ricky Torres.

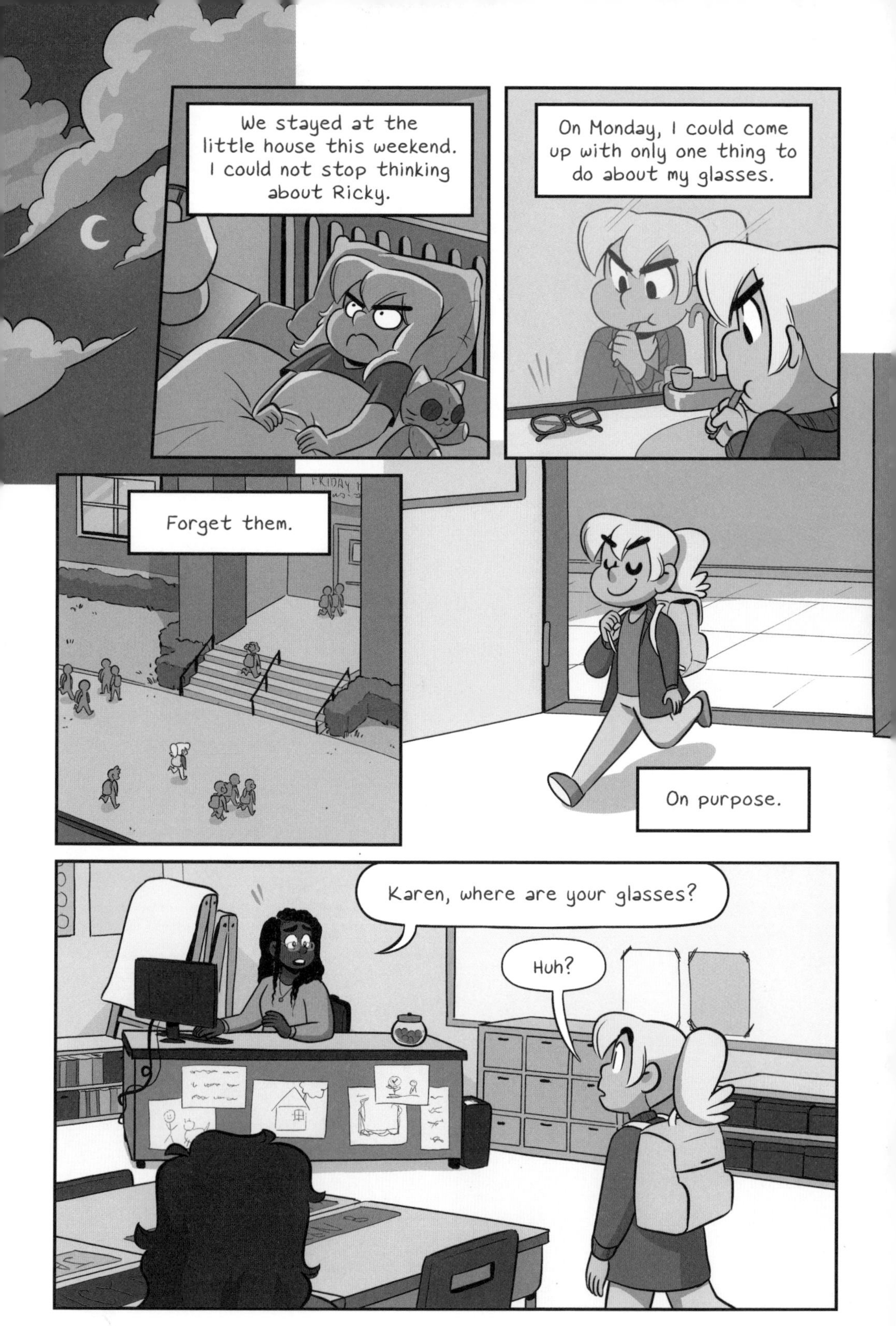
We stayed at the little house this weekend. I could not stop thinking about Ricky.
On Monday, I could come up with only one thing to do about my glasses.
Forget them.
On purpose.
Karen, where are your glasses?
Huh?

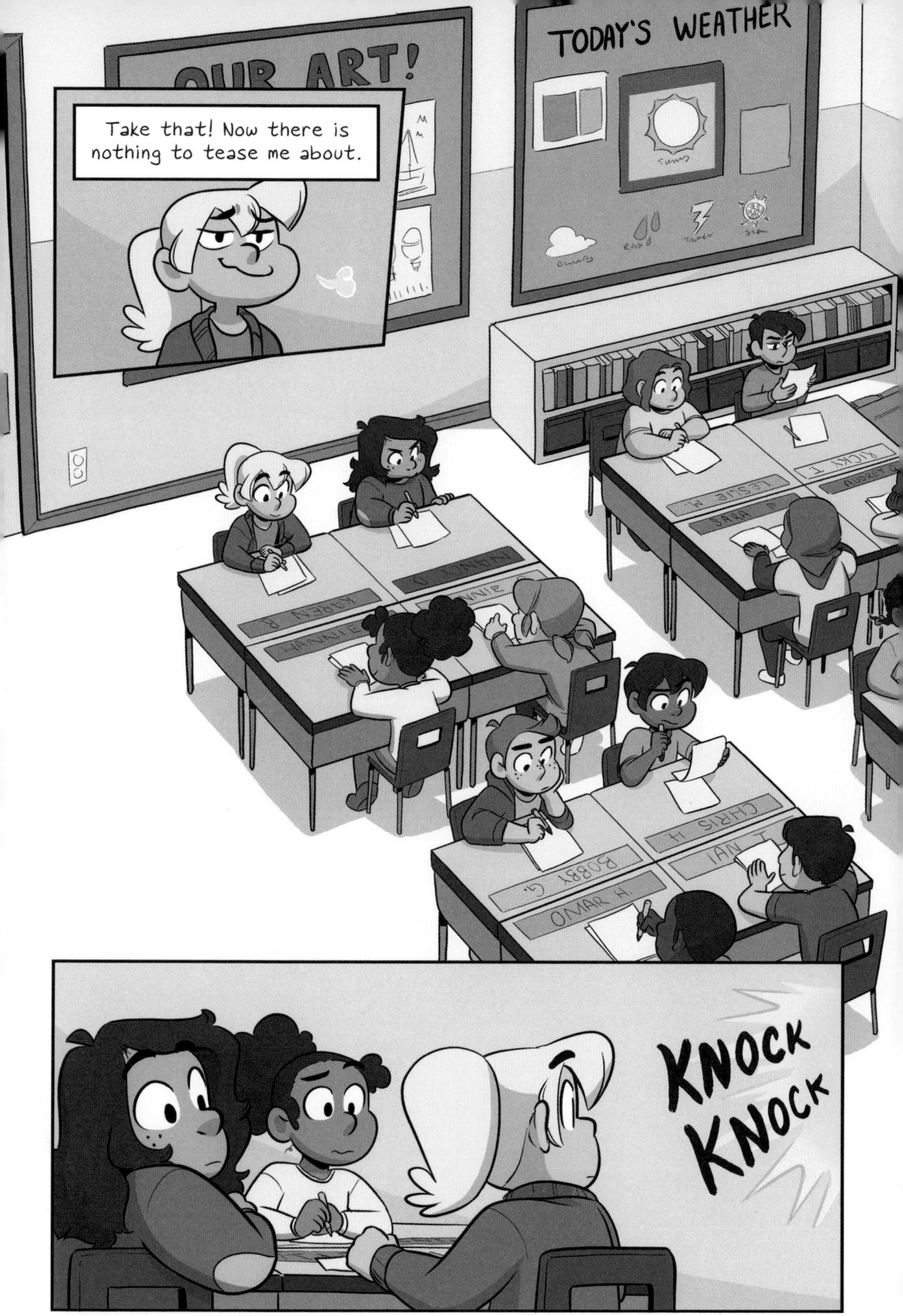
OUR ART!
TODAY'S WEATHER
Take that! Now there is nothing to tease me about.
KAREN B
HANNIE
LESLIE M.
RICKY T
SARA P
CHRIS H
IAN T
BOBBY G.
OMAR H.
KNOCK KNOCK

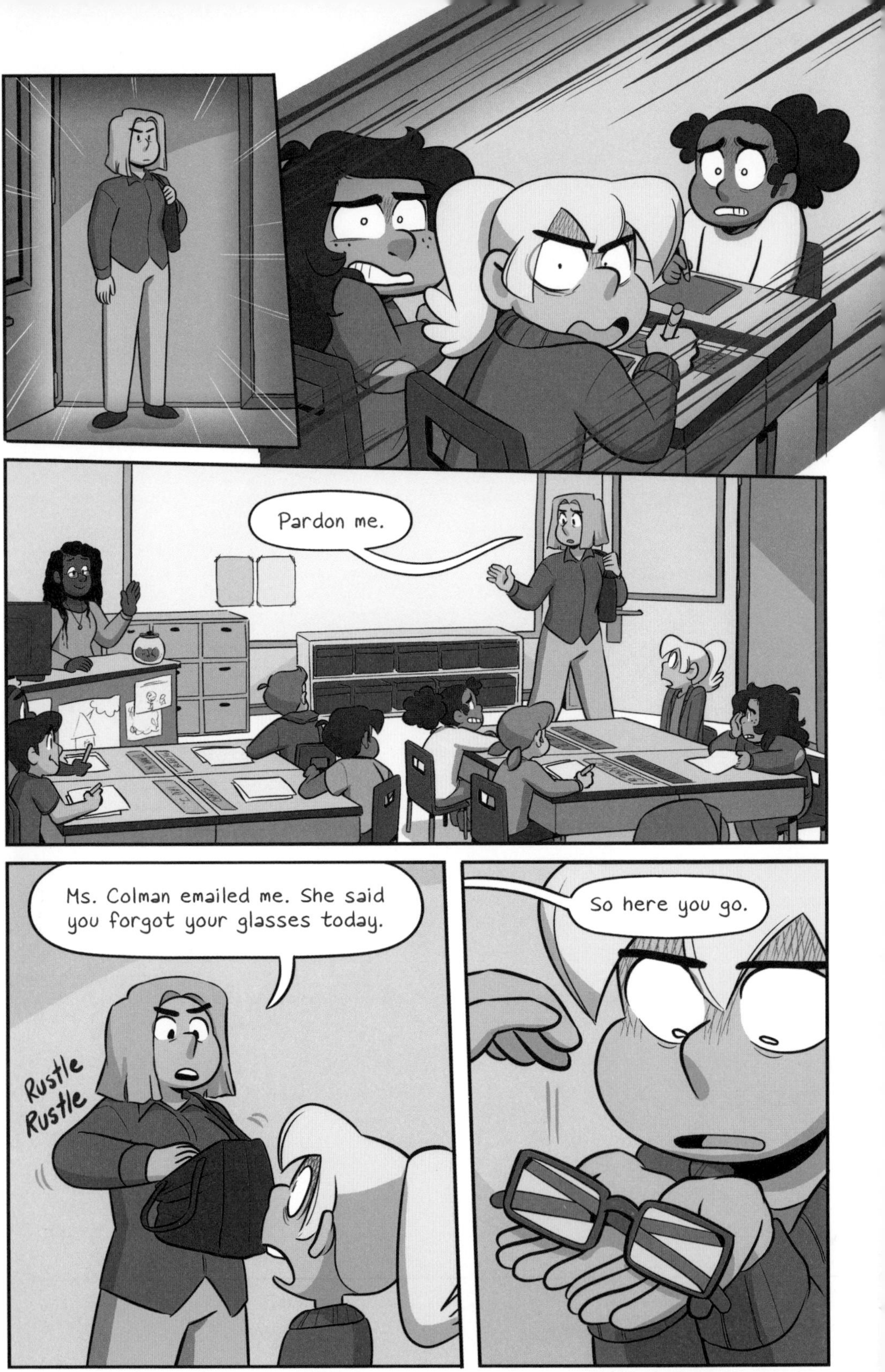
Pardon me.
Ms. Colman emailed me. She said you forgot your glasses today.
Rustle Rustle
So here you go.

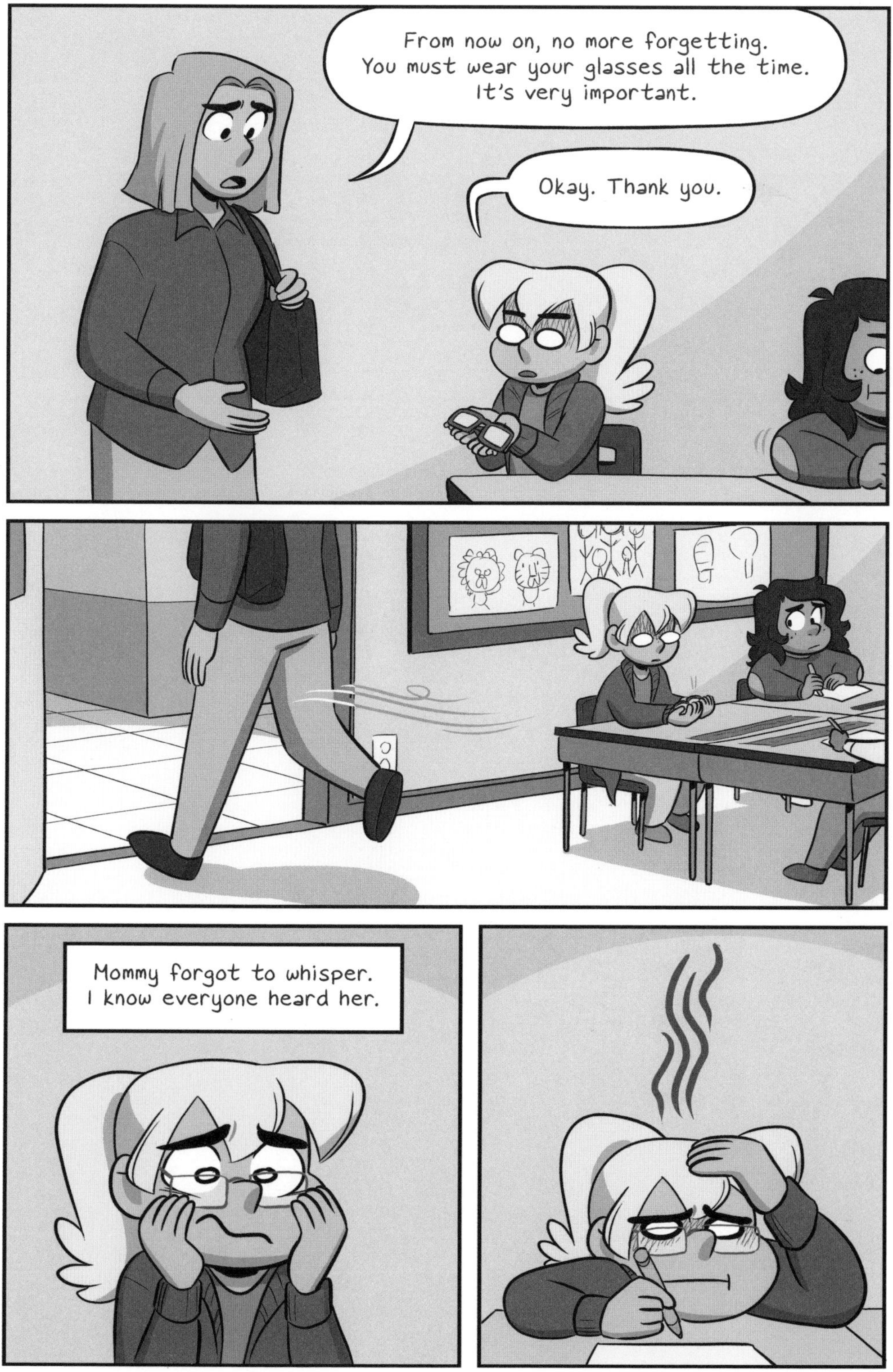
From now on, no more forgetting. You must wear your glasses all the time. It's very important.
Okay. Thank you.
Mommy forgot to whisper. I know everyone heard her.

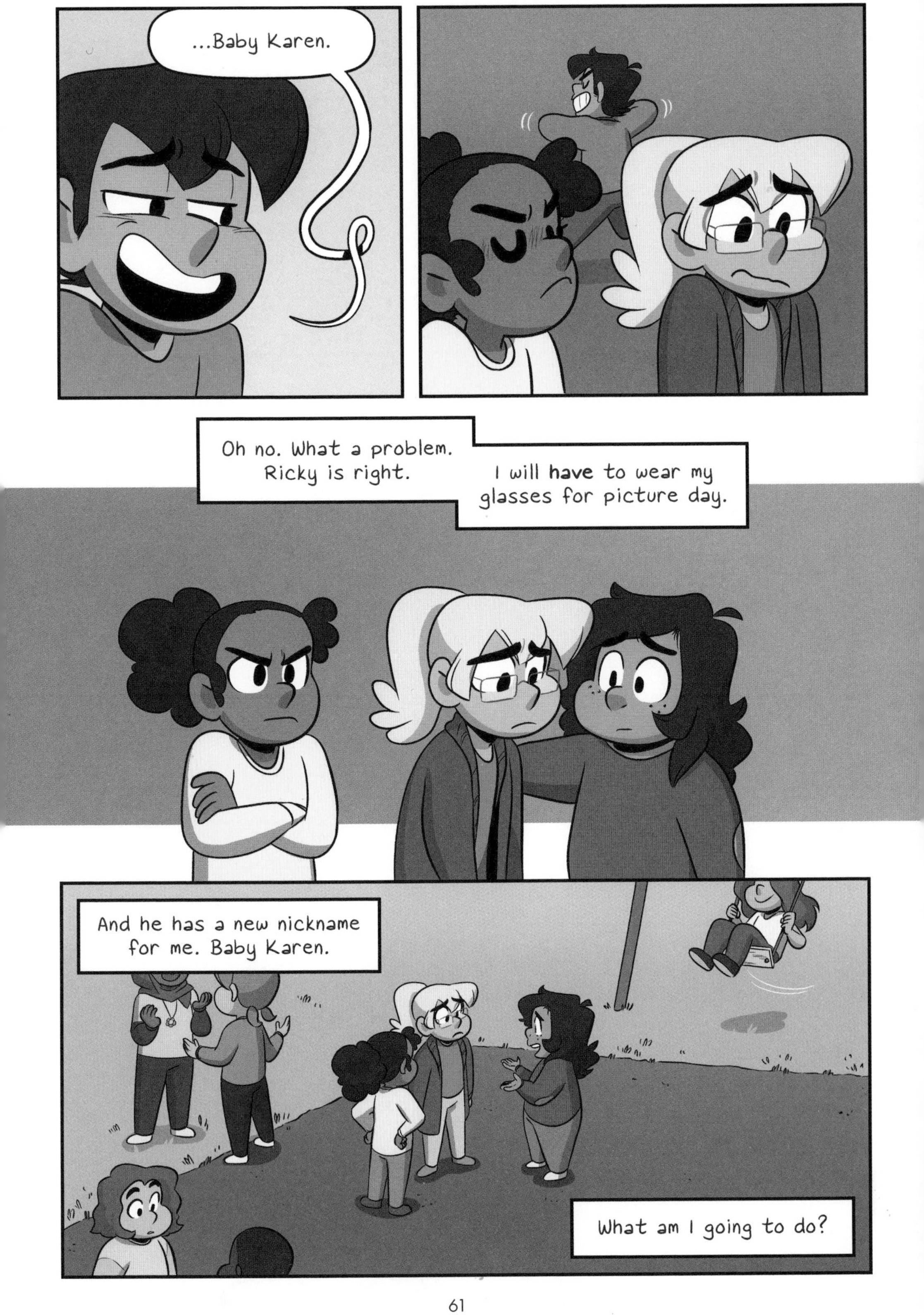
...Baby Karen.
Oh no. What a problem. Ricky is right.
I will **have** to wear my glasses for picture day.
And he has a new nickname for me. Baby Karen.
What am I going to do?

CHAPTER 6

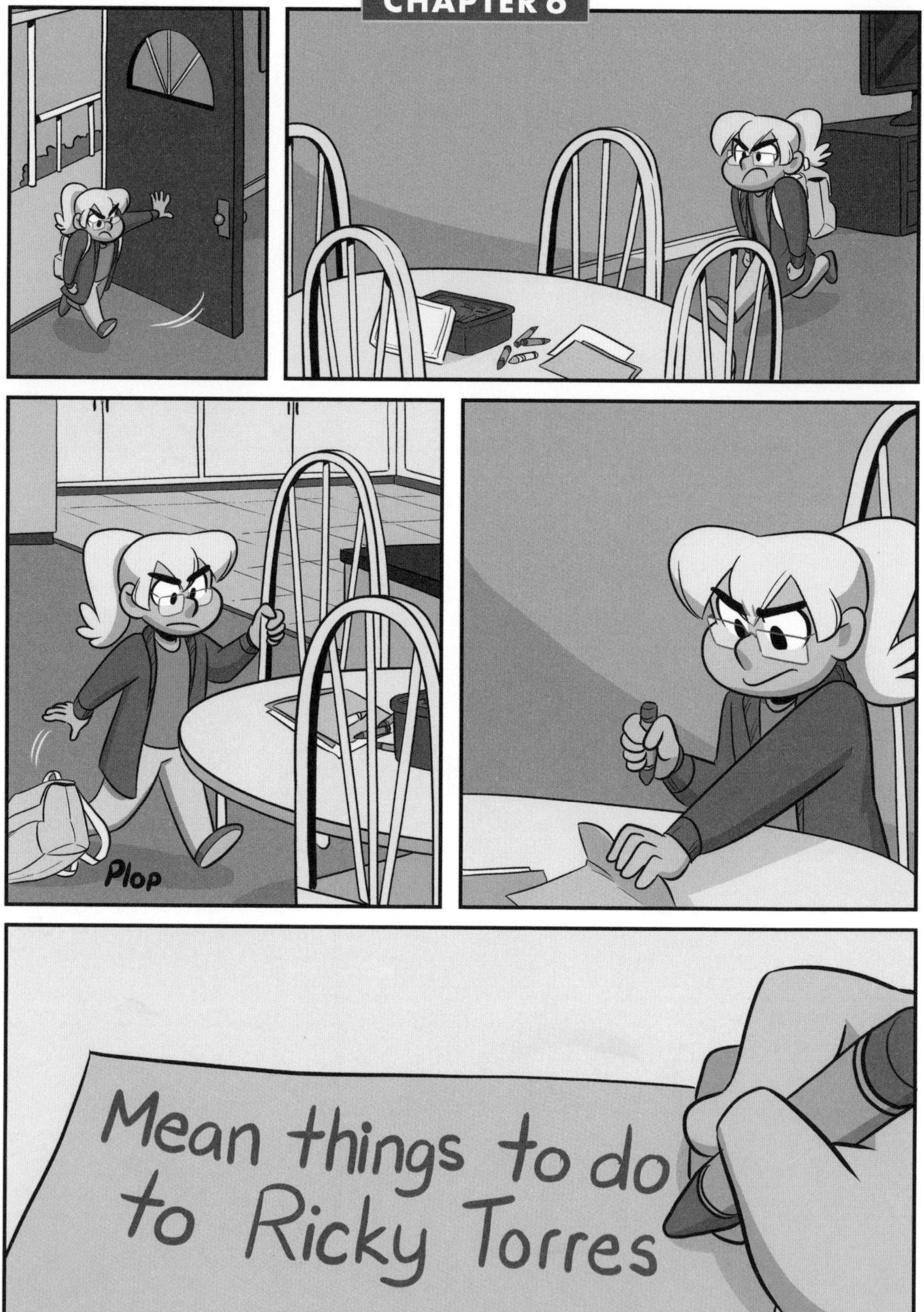
Plop
Mean things to do to Ricky Torres

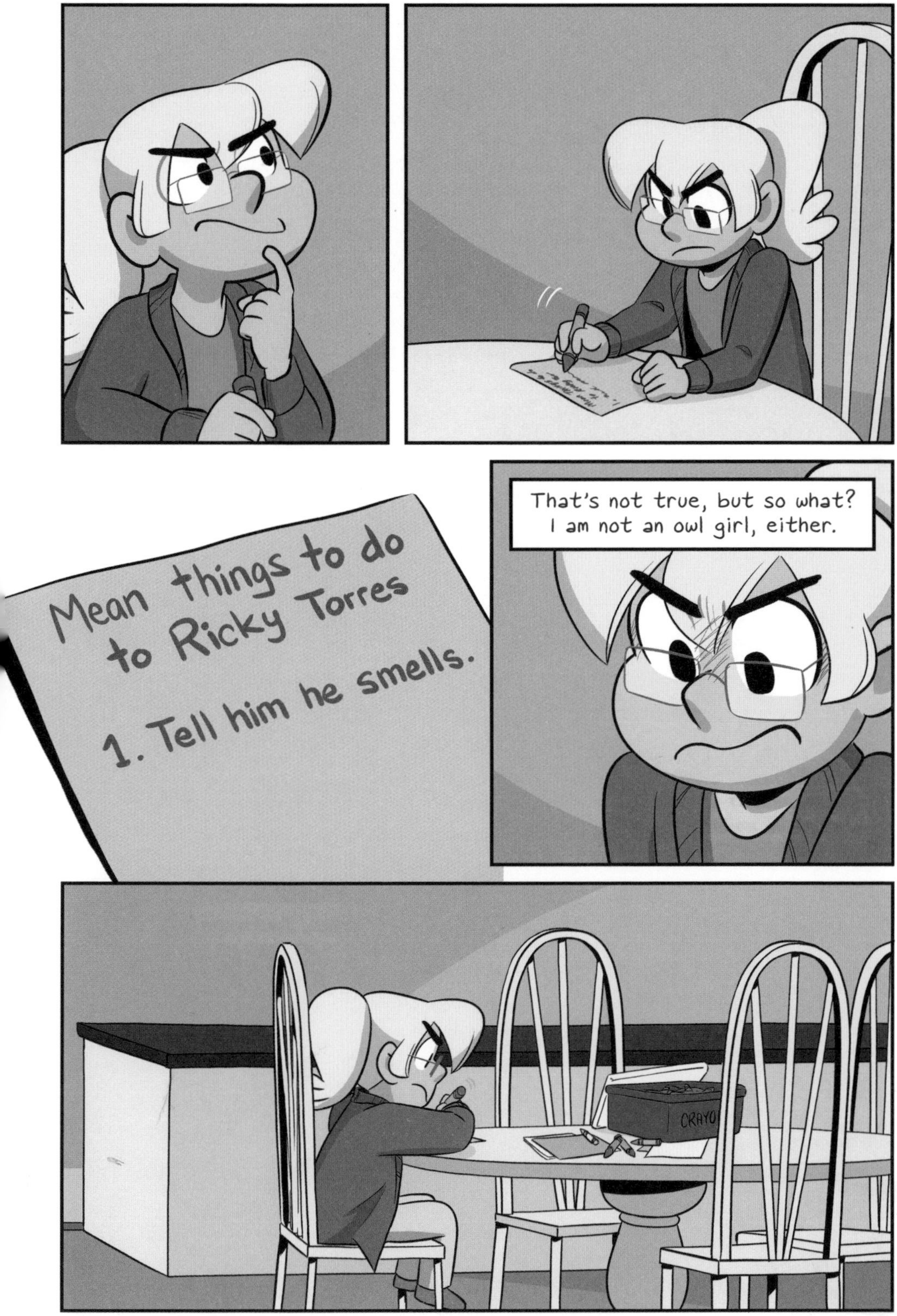
Mean things to do
to Ricky Torres
1. Tell him he smells.
That's not true, but so what?
I am not an owl girl, either.
CRAYO

64

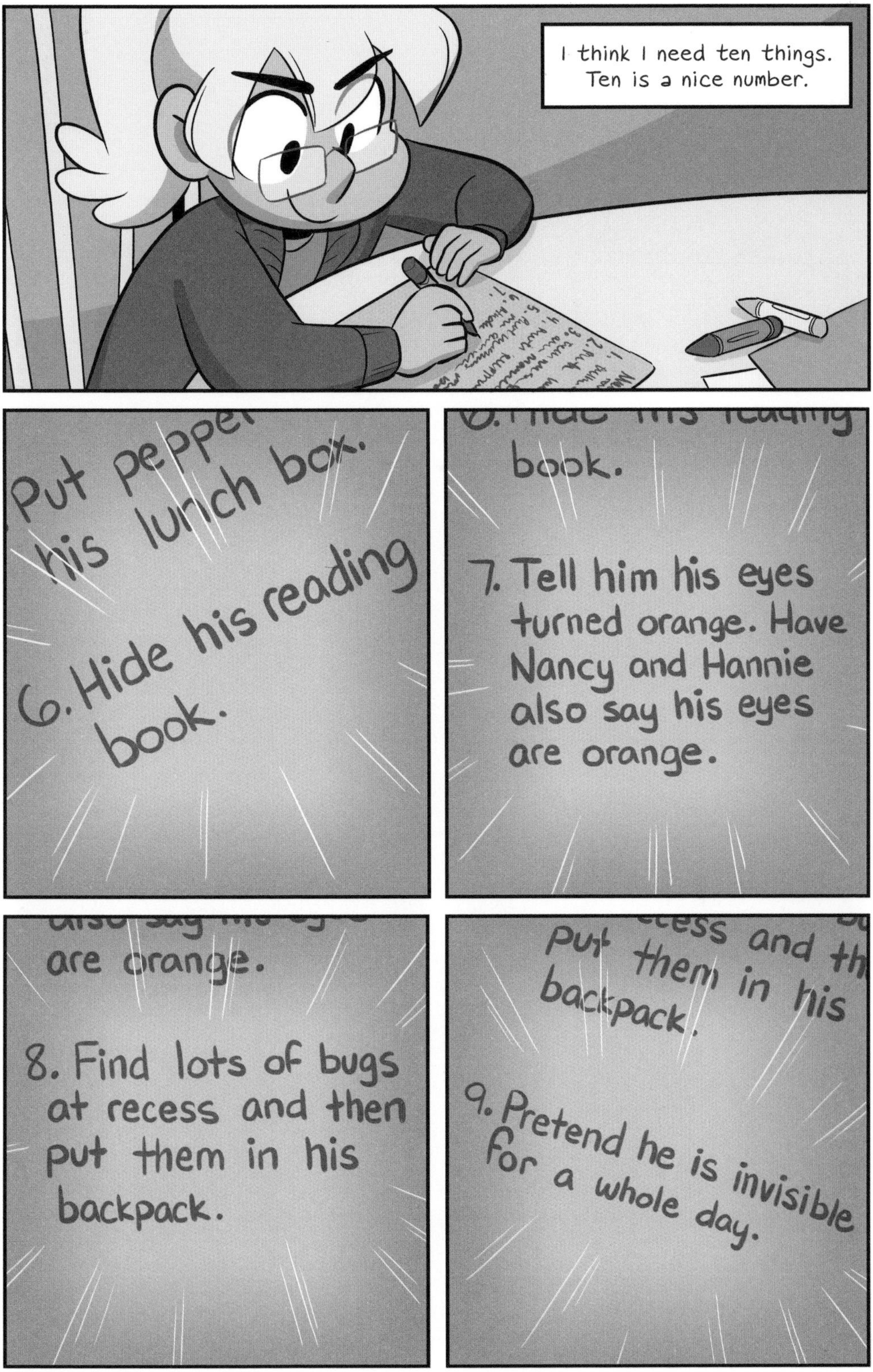
I think I need ten things. Ten is a nice number.
his lunch box.
6. Hide his reading book.
book.
7. Tell him his eyes turned orange. Have Nancy and Hannie also say his eyes are orange.
are orange.
8. Find lots of bugs at recess and then put them in his backpack.
put them in his backpack.
9. Pretend he is invisible for a whole day.

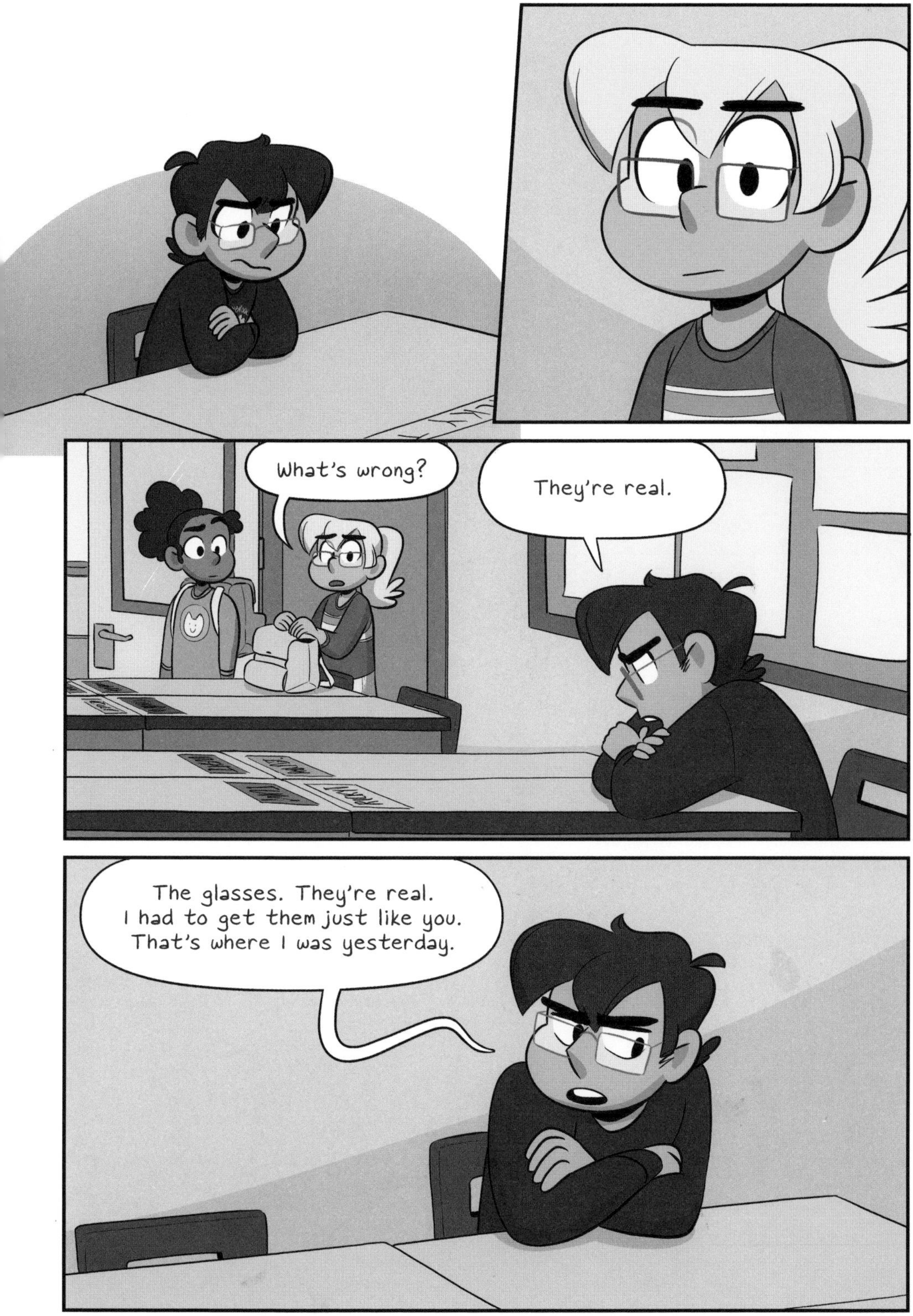
What's wrong?
They're real.
The glasses. They're real. I had to get them just like you. That's where I was yesterday.

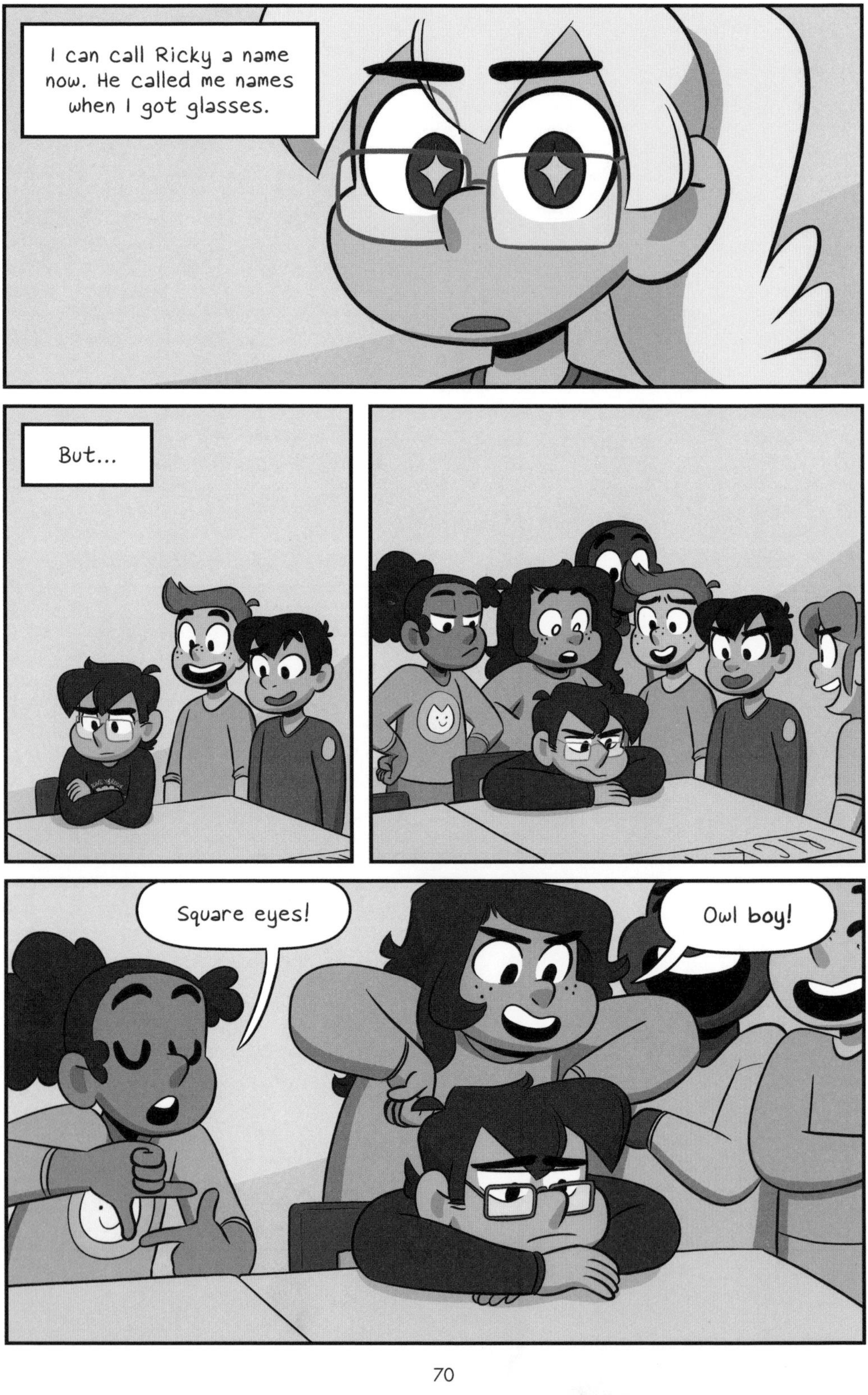
I can call Ricky a name now. He called me names when I got glasses.
But...
Square eyes!
Owl boy!

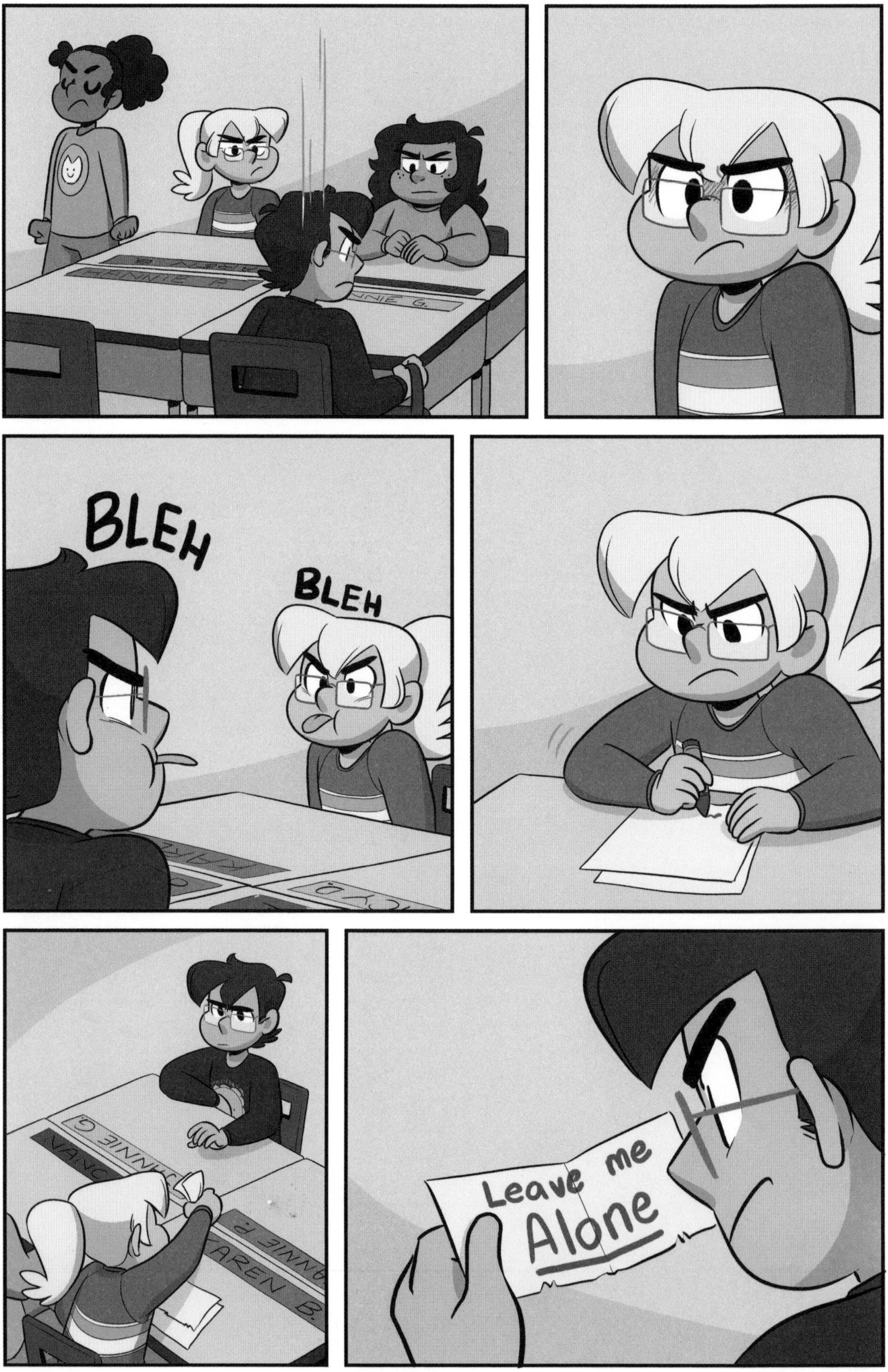
BLEH
BLEH
Leave me
Alone

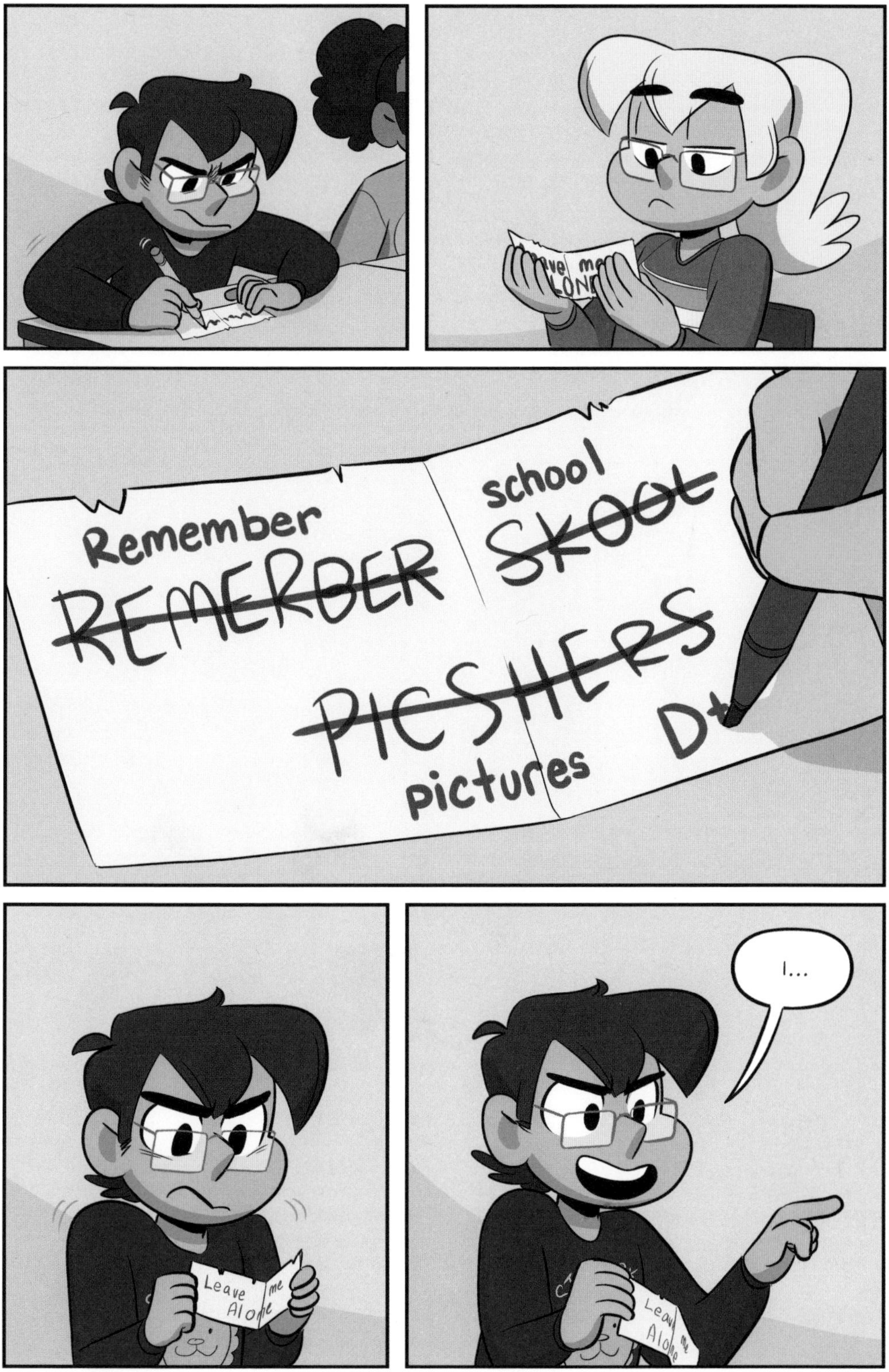
Leave me ALONE
Remember
REMERBER
school
SKOOL
PICSHERS
pictures
D+
Leave me Alone
I...
Leave me Alone

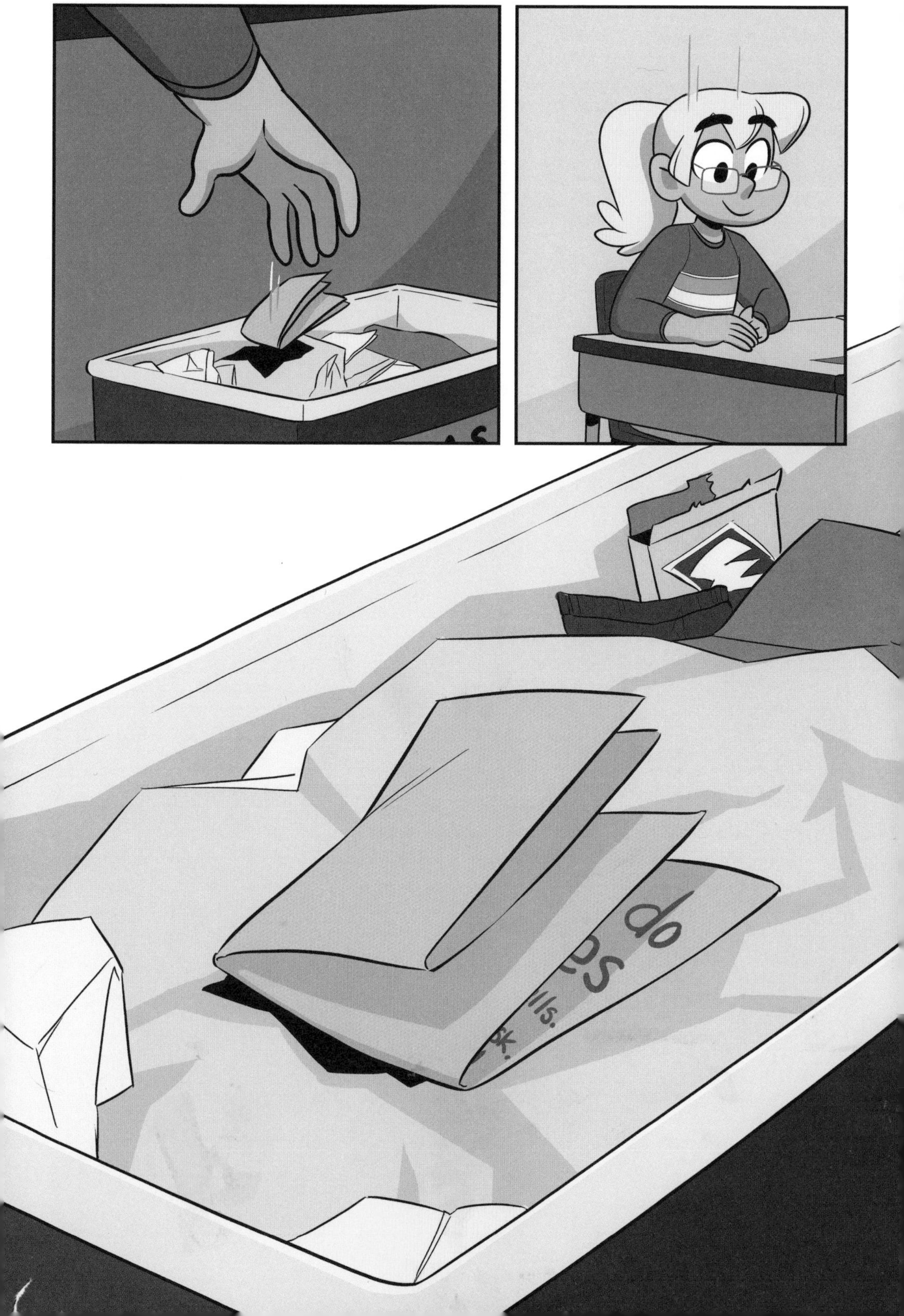

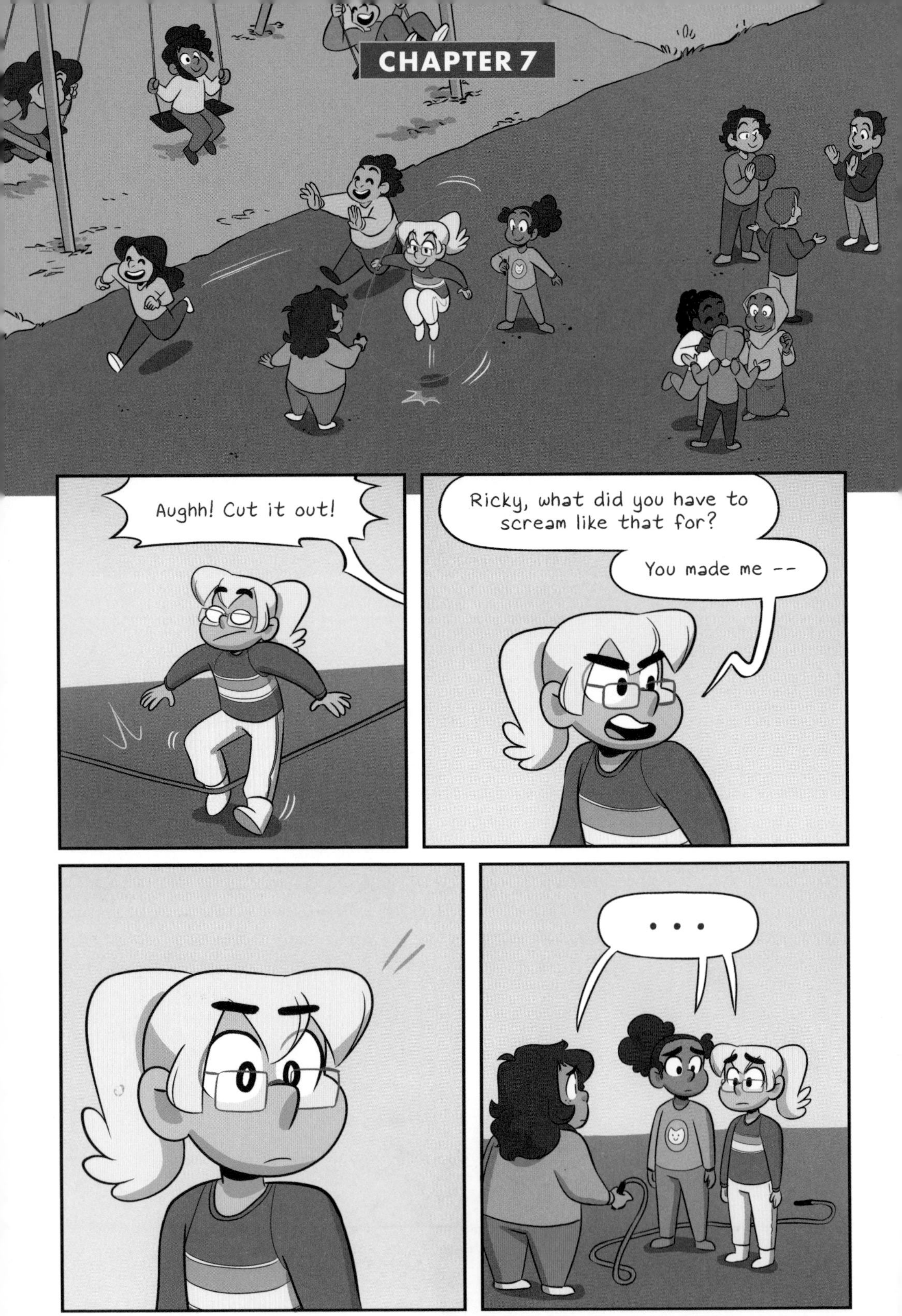
CHAPTER 7
Aughh! Cut it out!
Ricky, what did you have to scream like that for?
You made me --
. . .

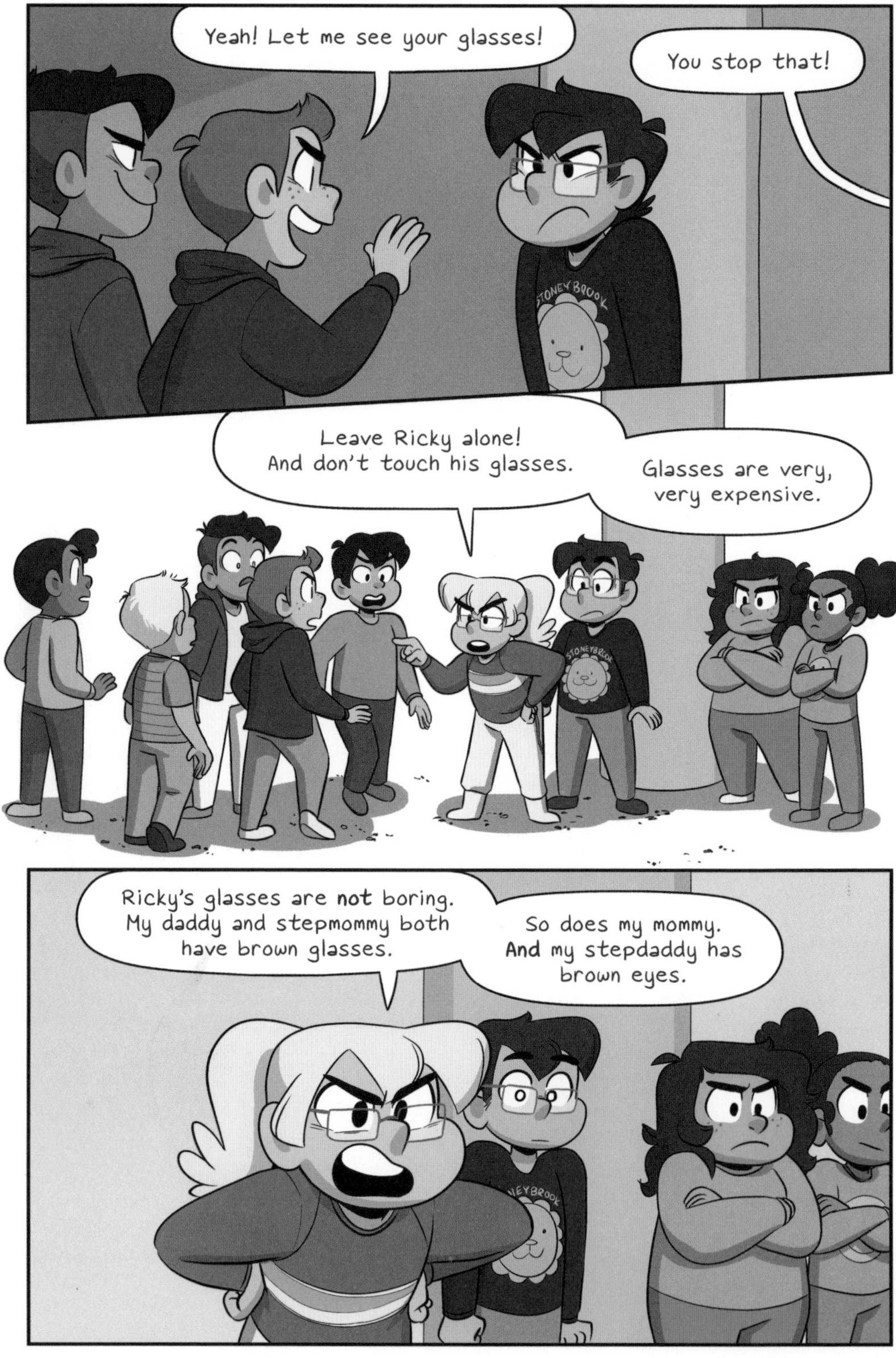
Yeah! Let me see your glasses!
You stop that!
STONEY BROOK
Leave Ricky alone!
And don't touch his glasses.
Glasses are very,
very expensive.
STONEYBROOK
Ricky's glasses are **not** boring.
My daddy and stepmommy both
have brown glasses.
So does my mommy.
And my stepdaddy has
brown eyes.
NEYBROOK

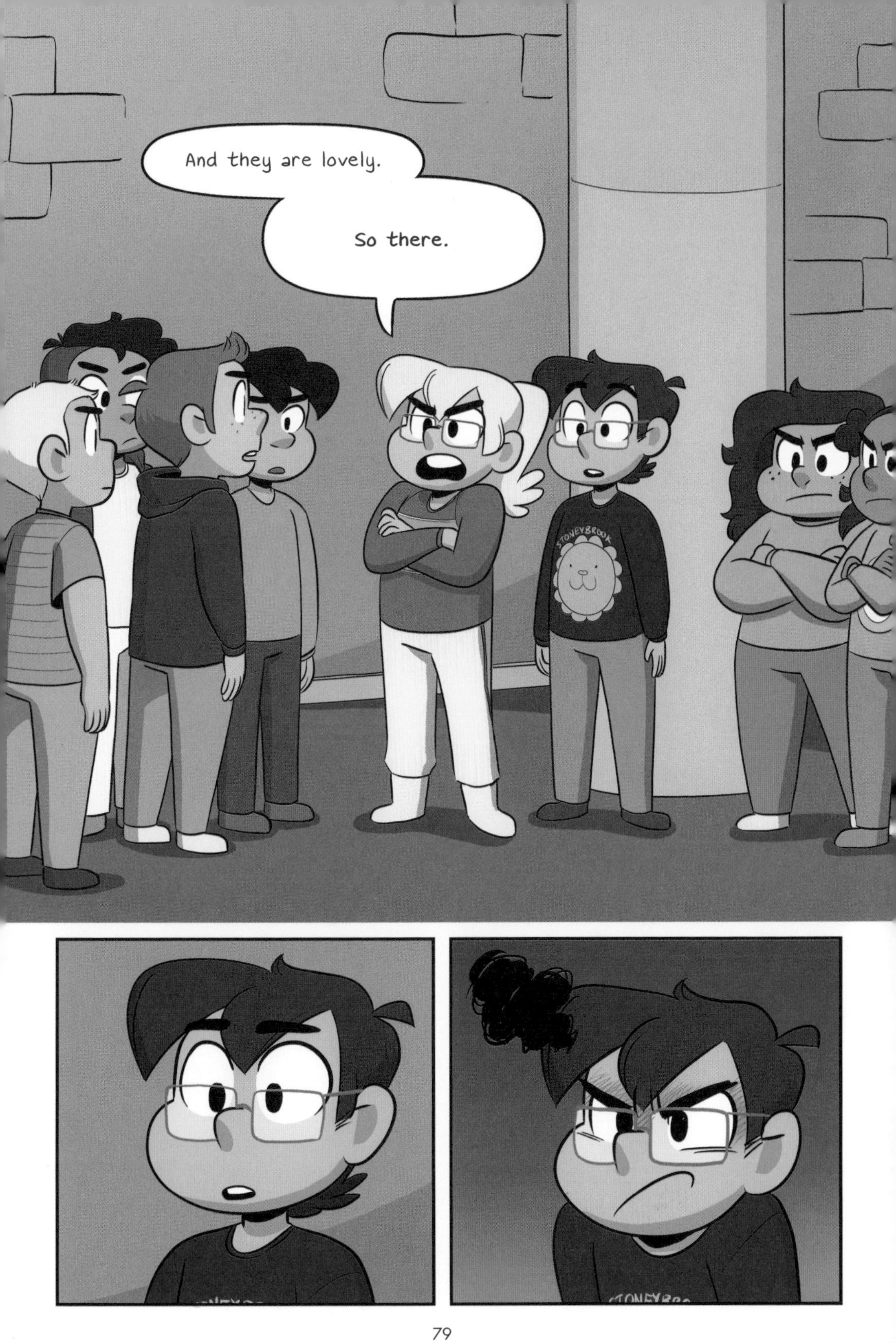
And they are lovely.
So there.
STONEYBROOK

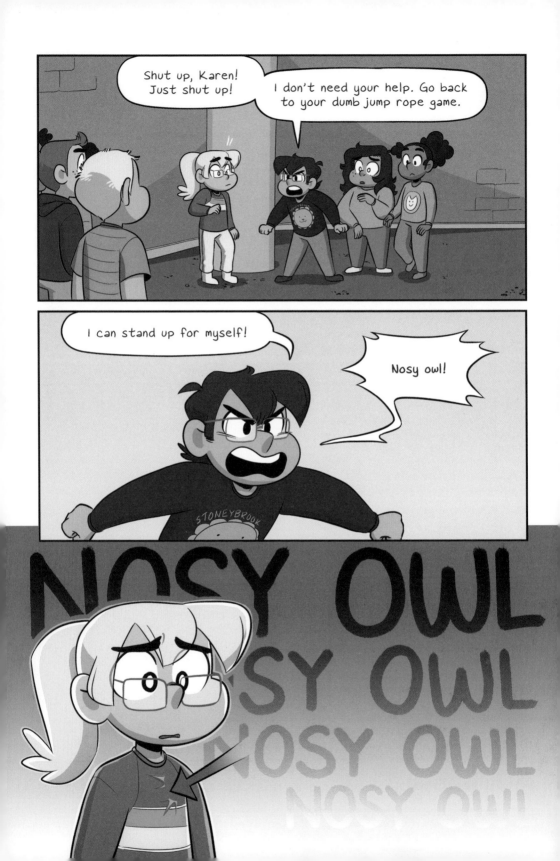

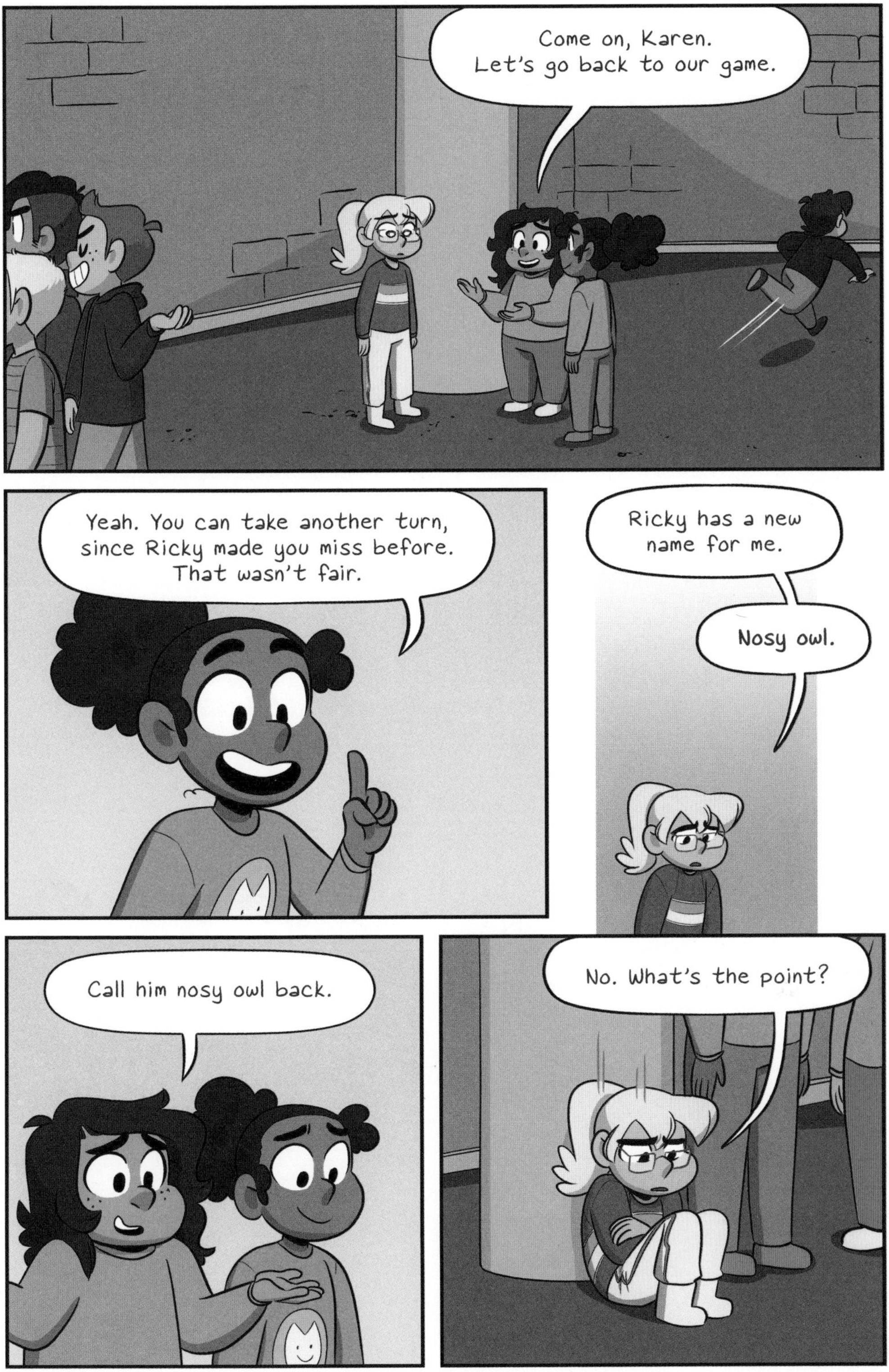
Come on, Karen.
Let's go back to our game.
Yeah. You can take another turn, since Ricky made you miss before. That wasn't fair.
Ricky has a new name for me.
Nosy owl.
Call him nosy owl back.
No. What's the point?

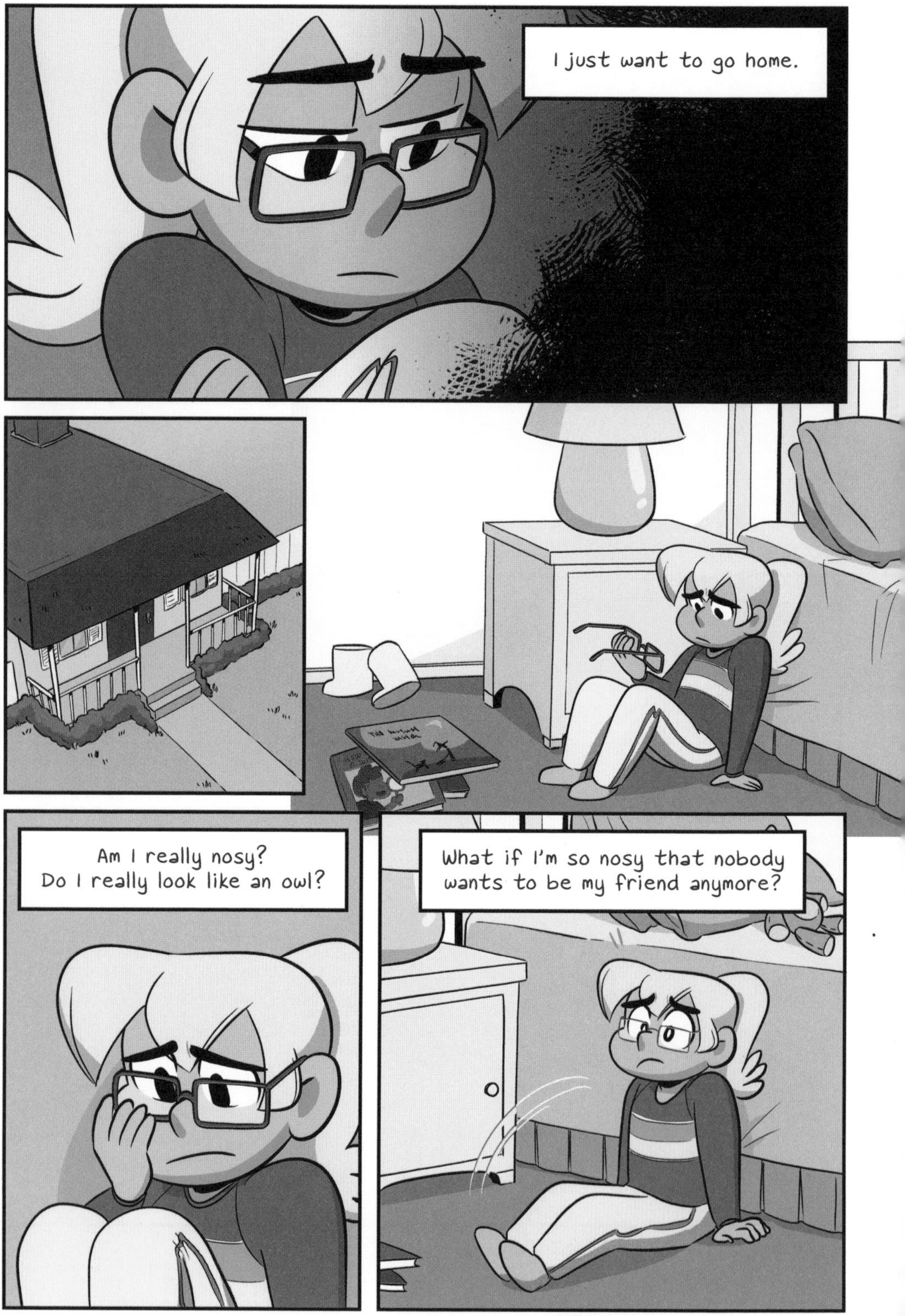
I just want to go home.
Am I really nosy?
Do I really look like an owl?
What if I'm so nosy that nobody wants to be my friend anymore?

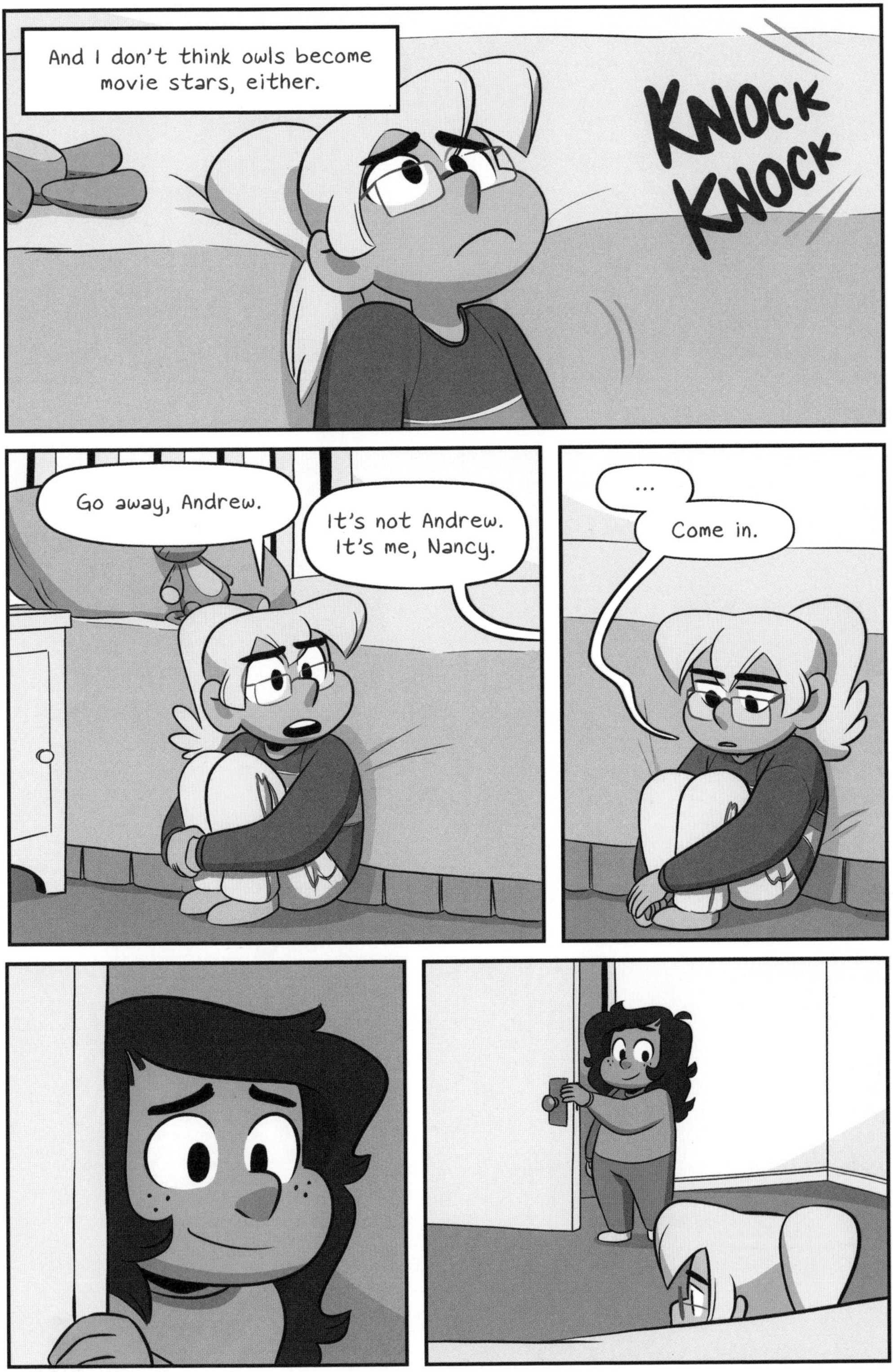
And I don't think owls become movie stars, either.
KNOCK KNOCK
Go away, Andrew.
It's not Andrew. It's me, Nancy.
...
Come in.

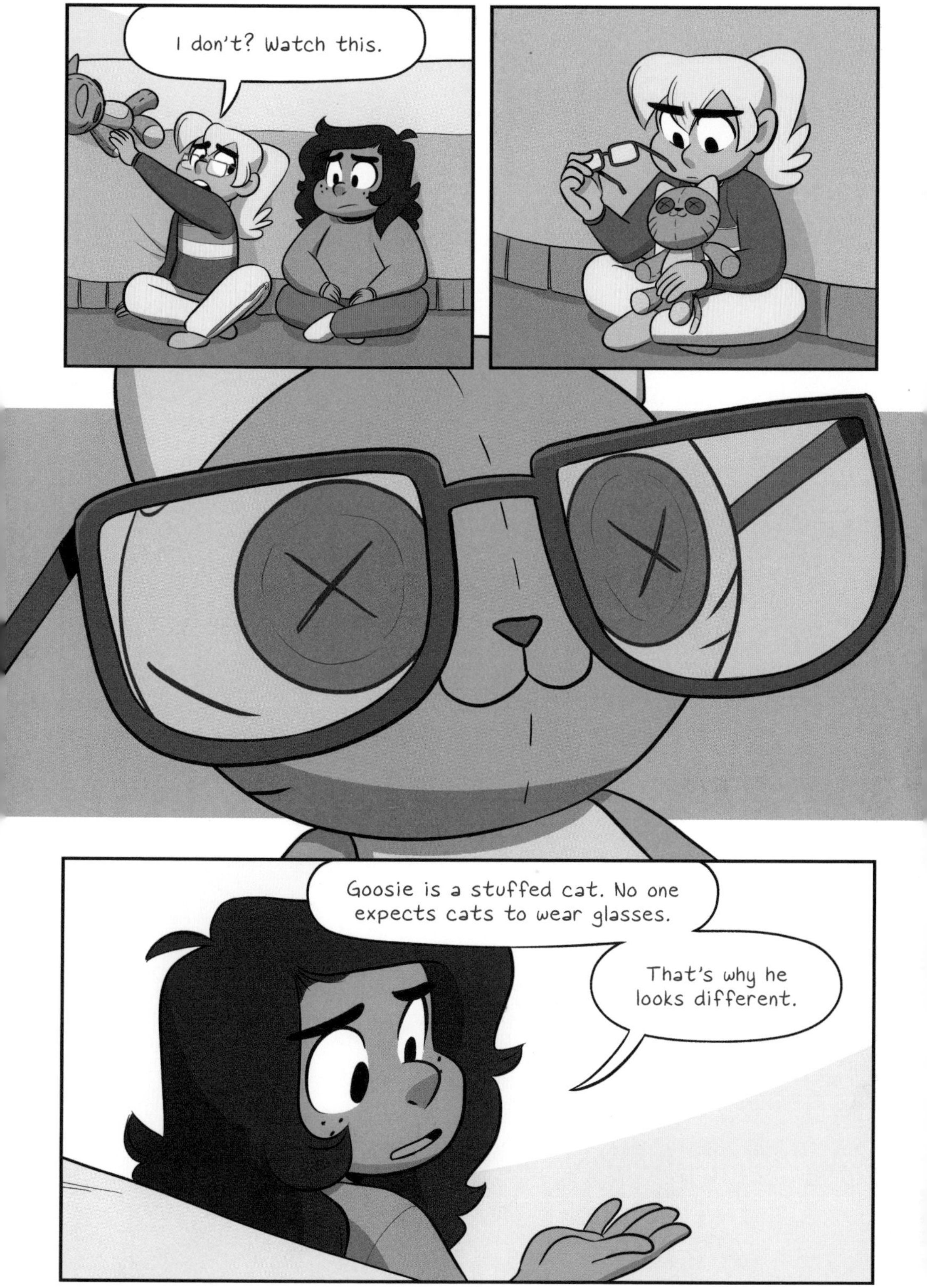
I don't? Watch this.
Goosie is a stuffed cat. No one expects cats to wear glasses.
That's why he looks different.

87

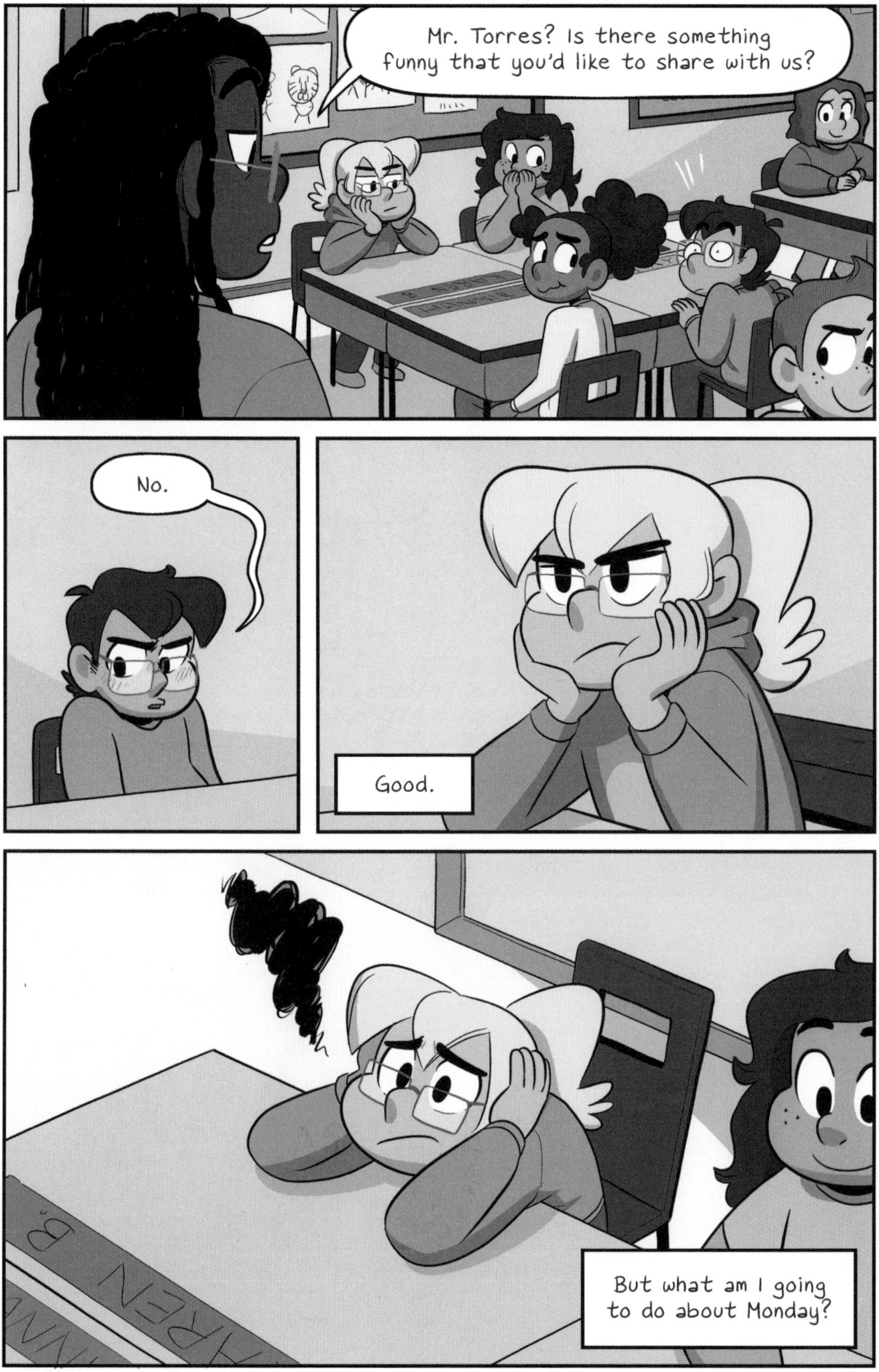

Mr. Torres? Is there something funny that you'd like to share with us?
No.
Good.
But what am I going to do about Monday?

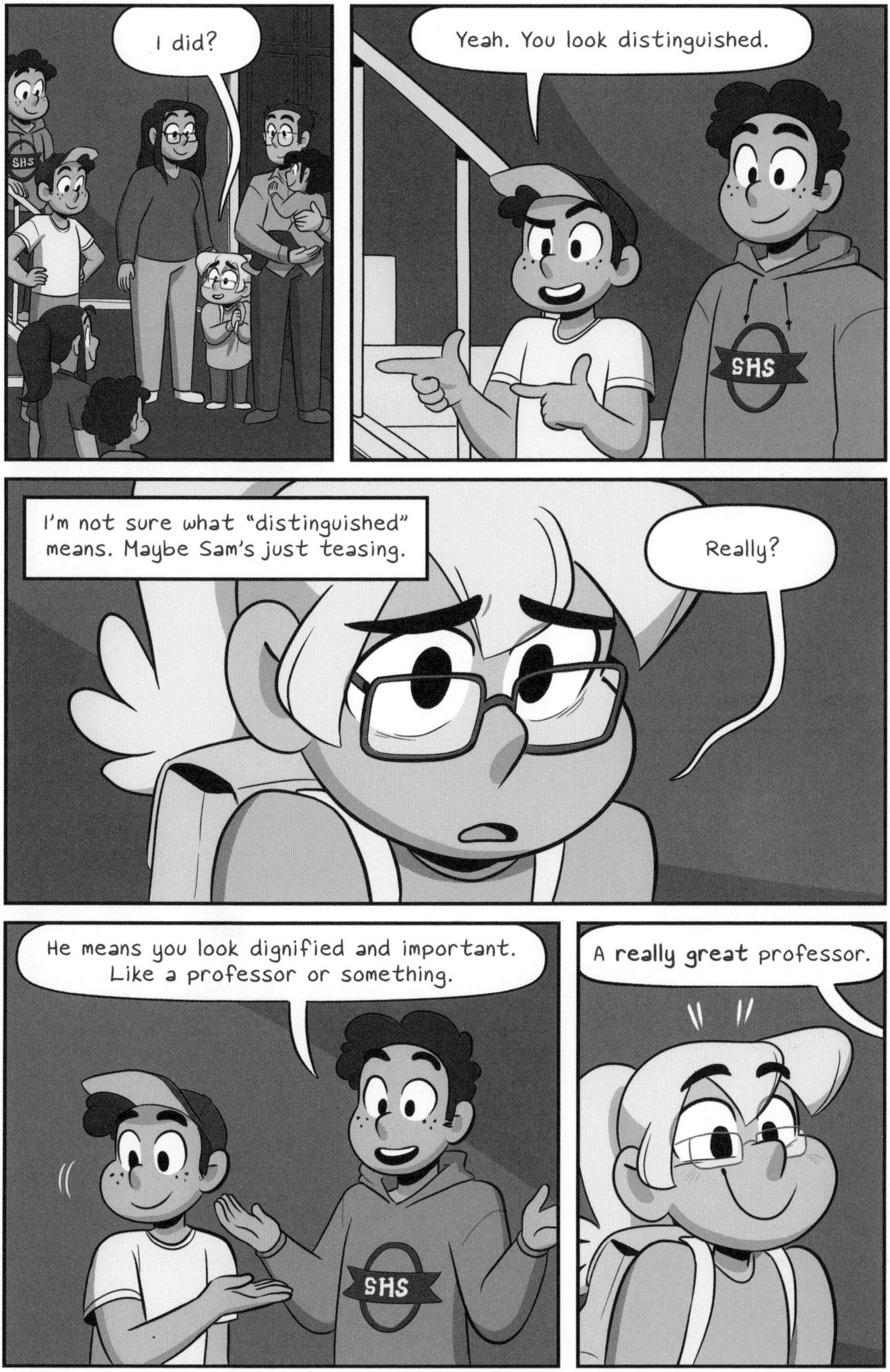
I did?
Yeah. You look distinguished.
SHS
I'm not sure what "distinguished" means. Maybe Sam's just teasing.
Really?
He means you look dignified and important. Like a professor or something.
SHS
A **really great** professor.

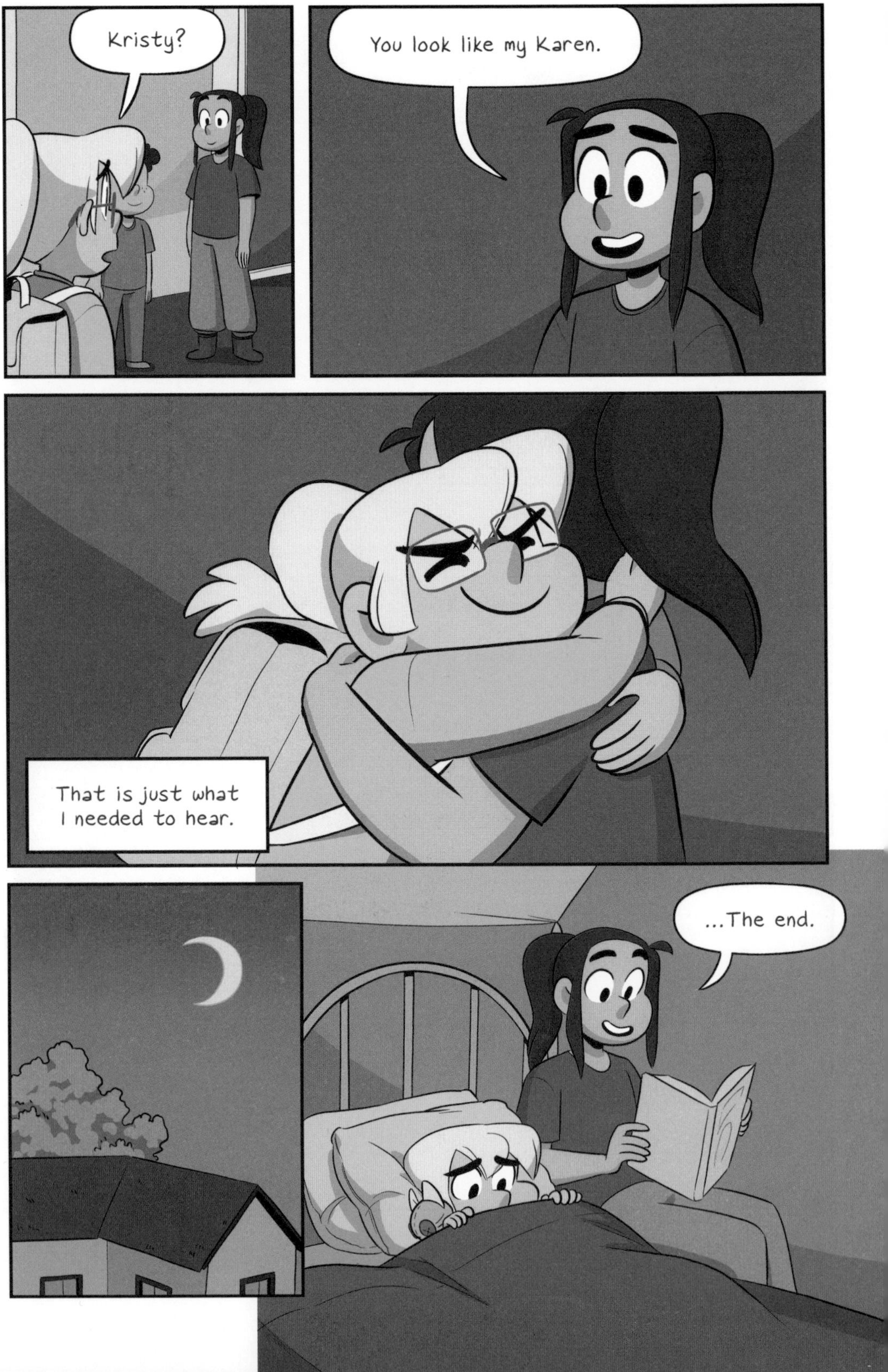
Kristy?
You look like my Karen.
That is just what I needed to hear.
...The end.

94

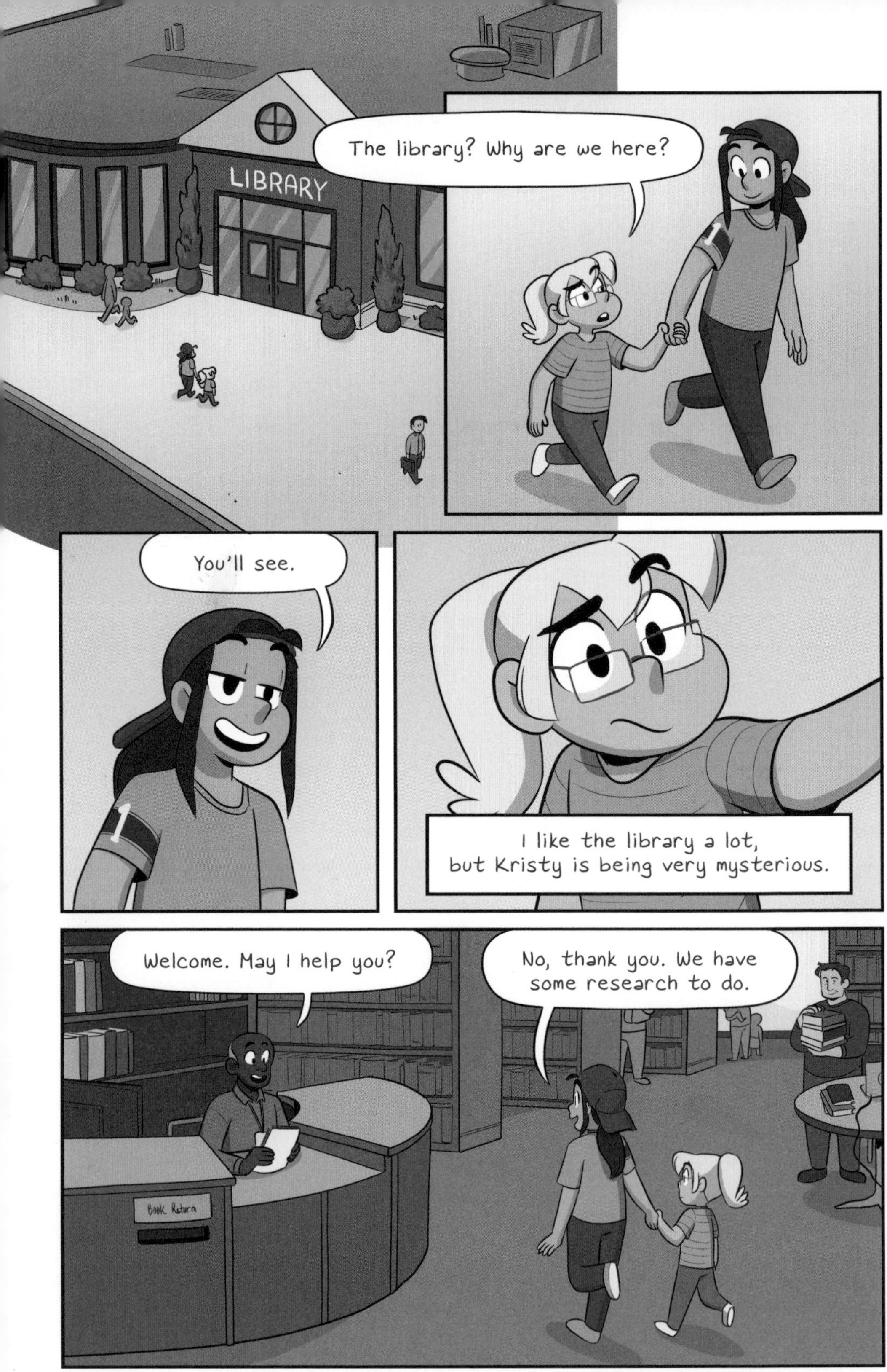
LIBRARY
The library? Why are we here?
You'll see.
I like the library a lot,
but Kristy is being very mysterious.
Welcome. May I help you?
No, thank you. We have
some research to do.
Book Return

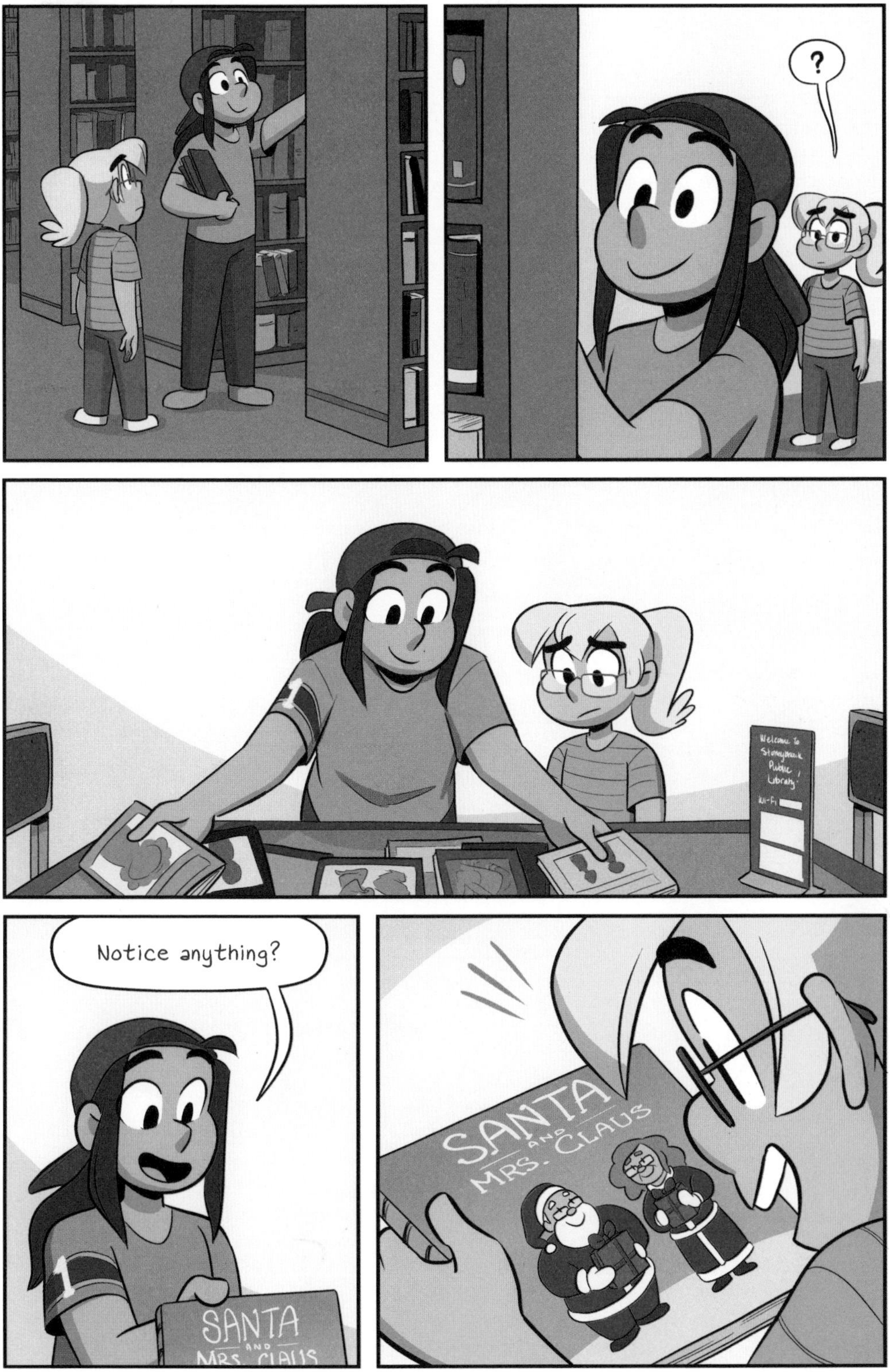
?
Welcome to Stoneybrook Public Library!
Wi-Fi
Notice anything?
SANTA AND MRS. CLAUS
SANTA AND MRS. CLAUS

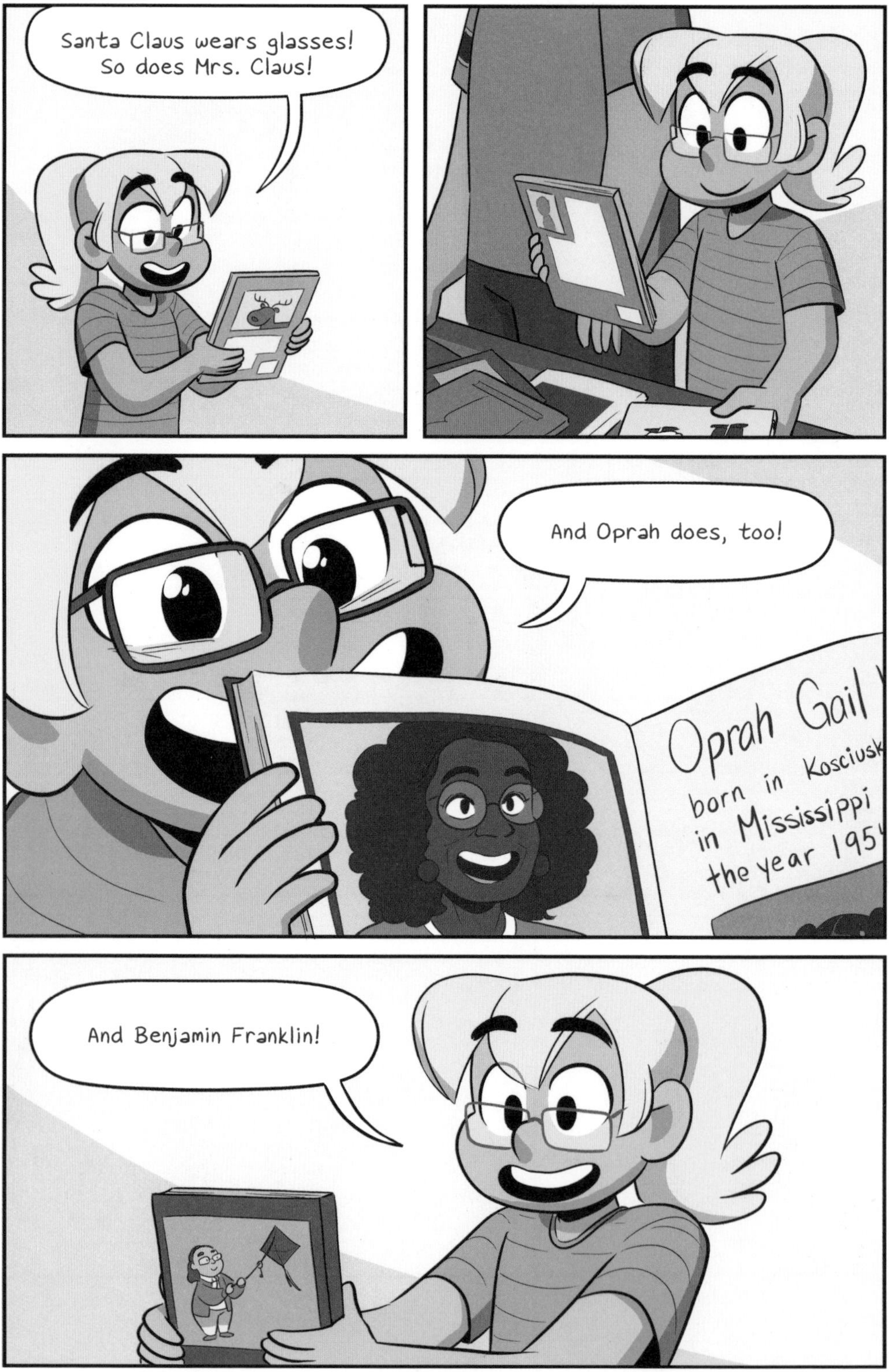
Santa Claus wears glasses! So does Mrs. Claus!
And Oprah does, too!
Oprah Gail
born in Kosciusk
in Mississippi
the year 195
And Benjamin Franklin!

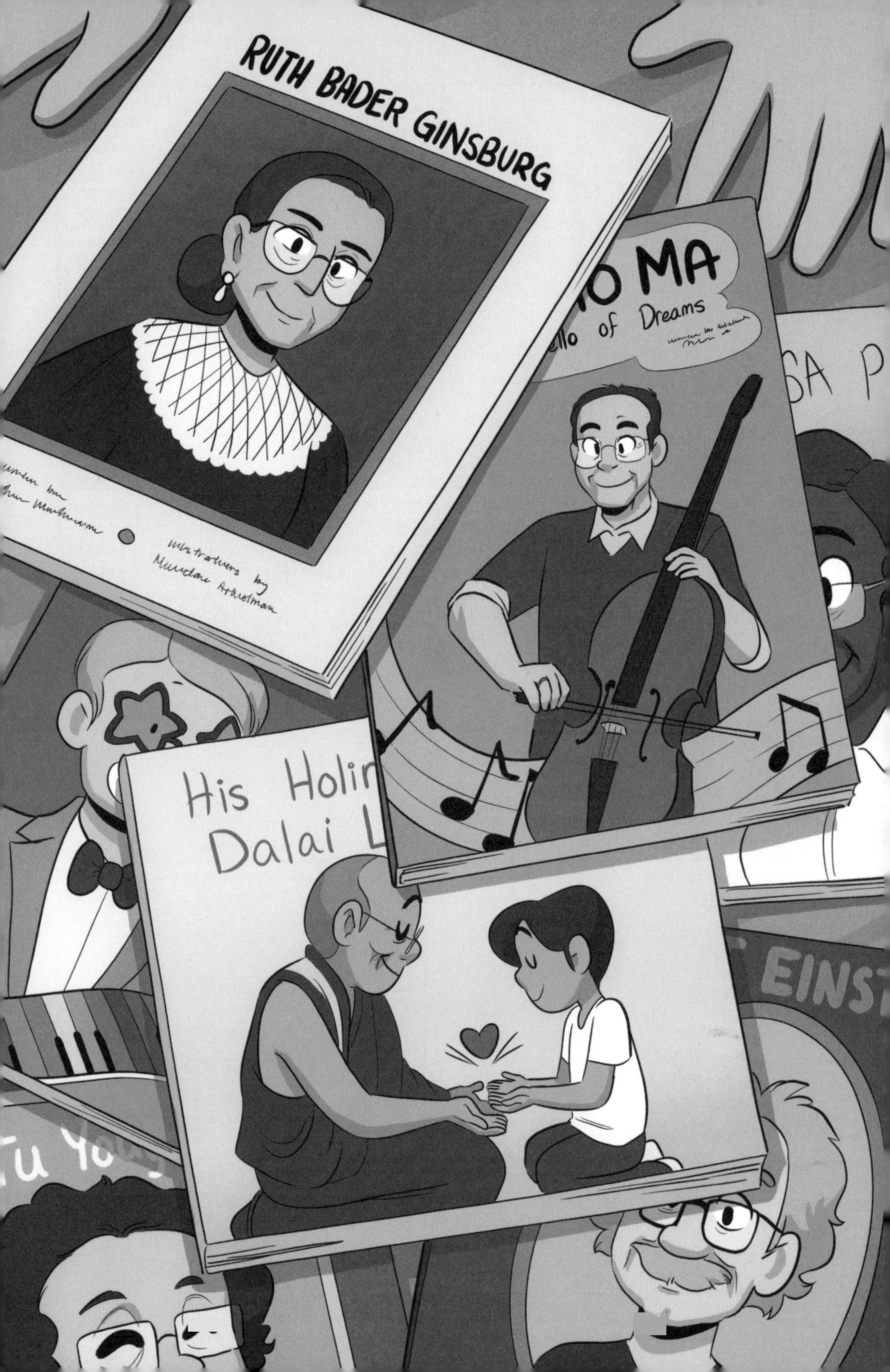
RUTH BADER GINSBURG
MA
ello of Dreams
SA P
His Holin
Dalai L
EINST
Tu You

CHAPTER 9

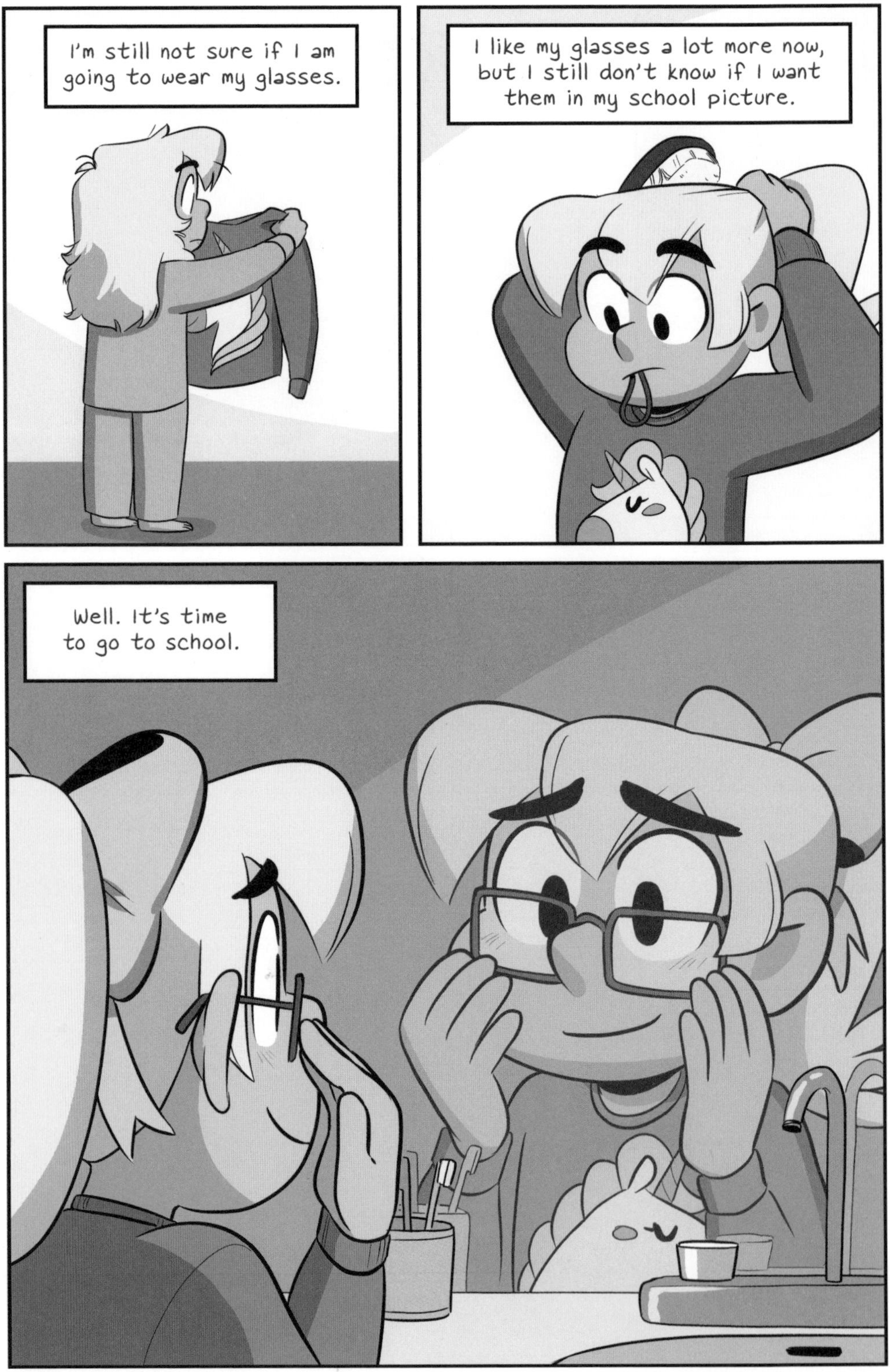
I'm still not sure if I am going to wear my glasses.
I like my glasses a lot more now, but I still don't know if I want them in my school picture.
Well. It's time to go to school.

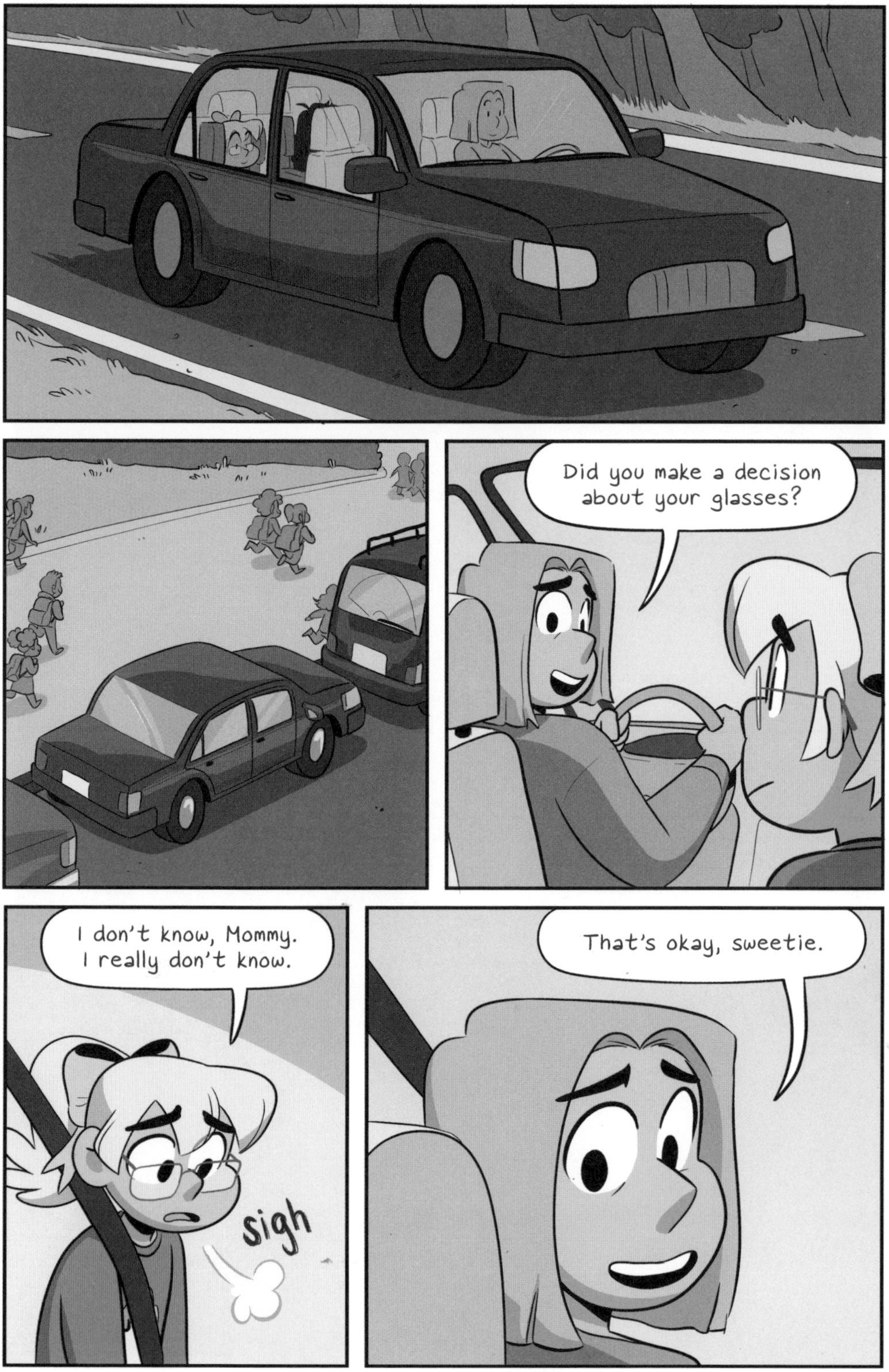
Did you make a decision about your glasses?
I don't know, Mommy. I really don't know.
sigh
That's okay, sweetie.

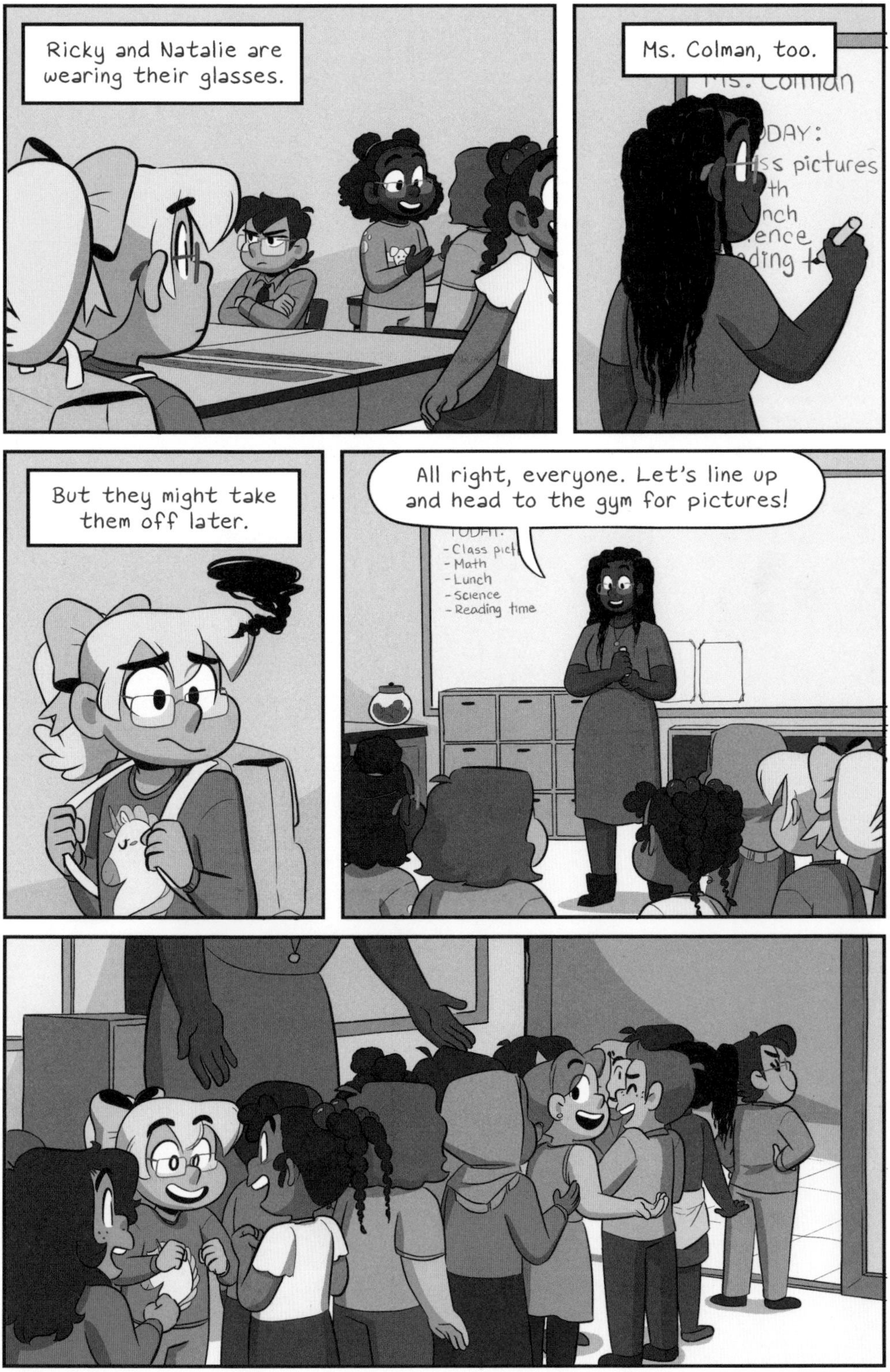
Ricky and Natalie are wearing their glasses.
Ms. Colman, too.
But they might take them off later.
All right, everyone. Let's line up and head to the gym for pictures!
- Math
- Lunch
- Science
- Reading time

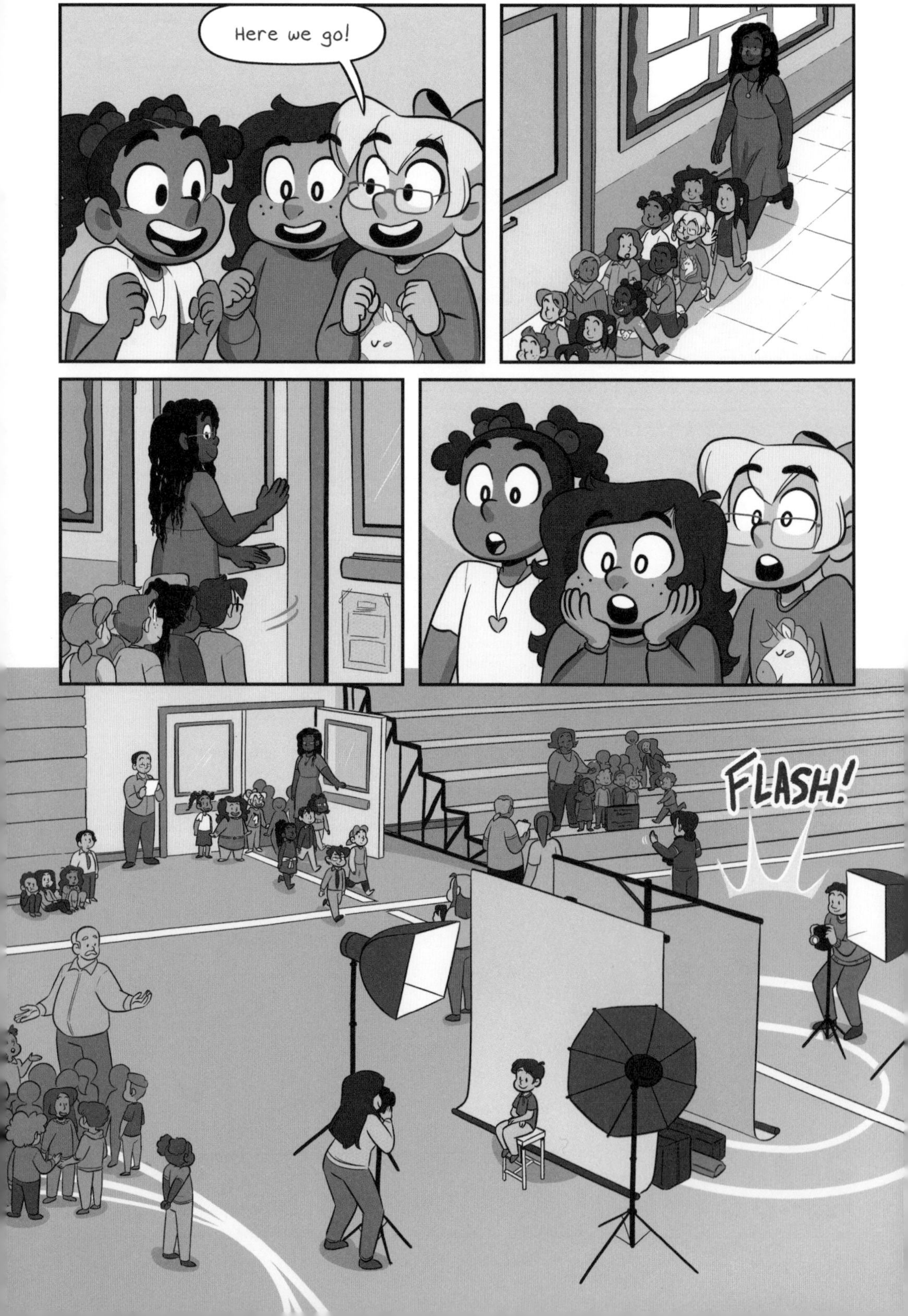
Here we go!
FLASH!

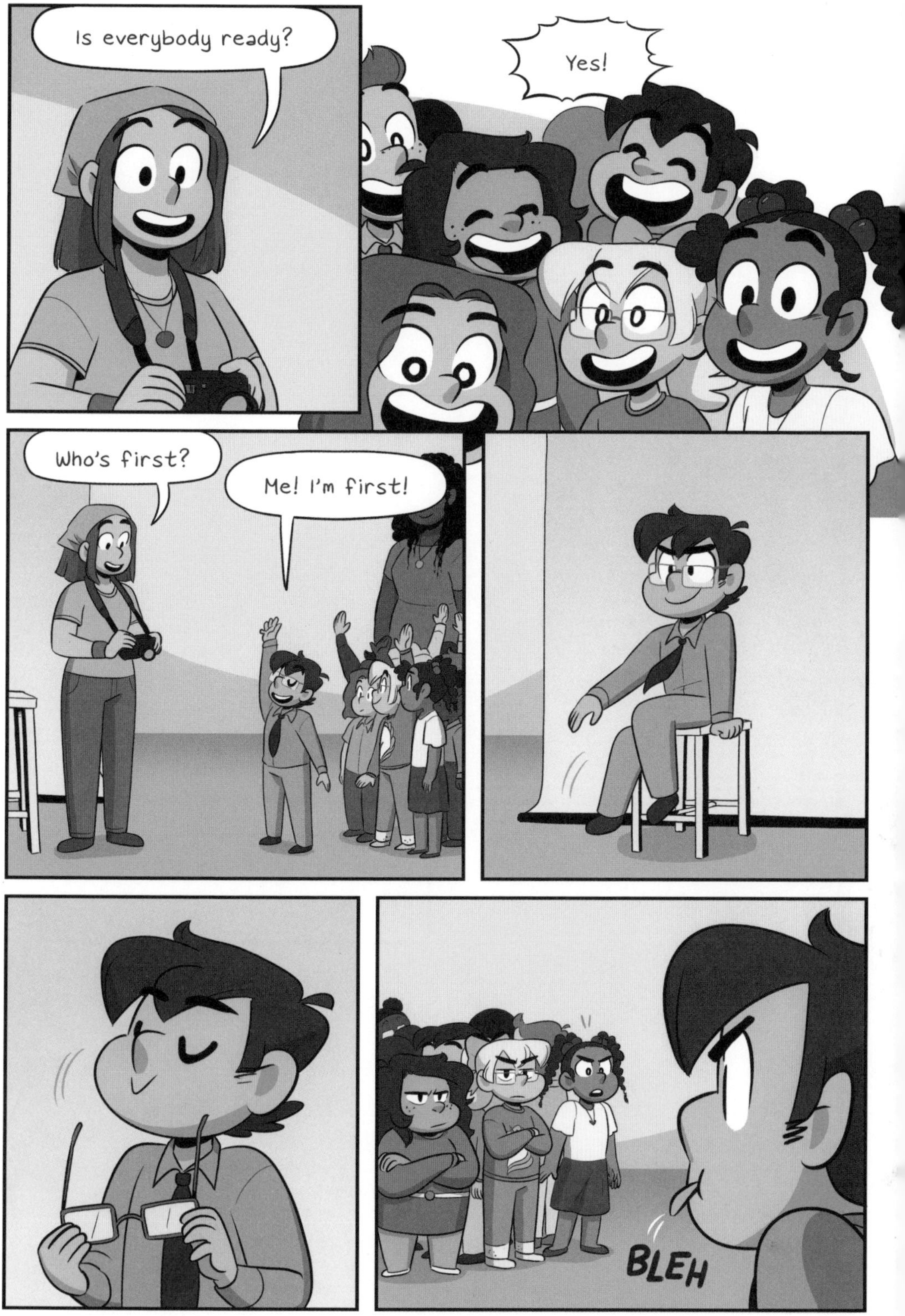
Is everybody ready?
Yes!
Who's first?
Me! I'm first!
BLEH

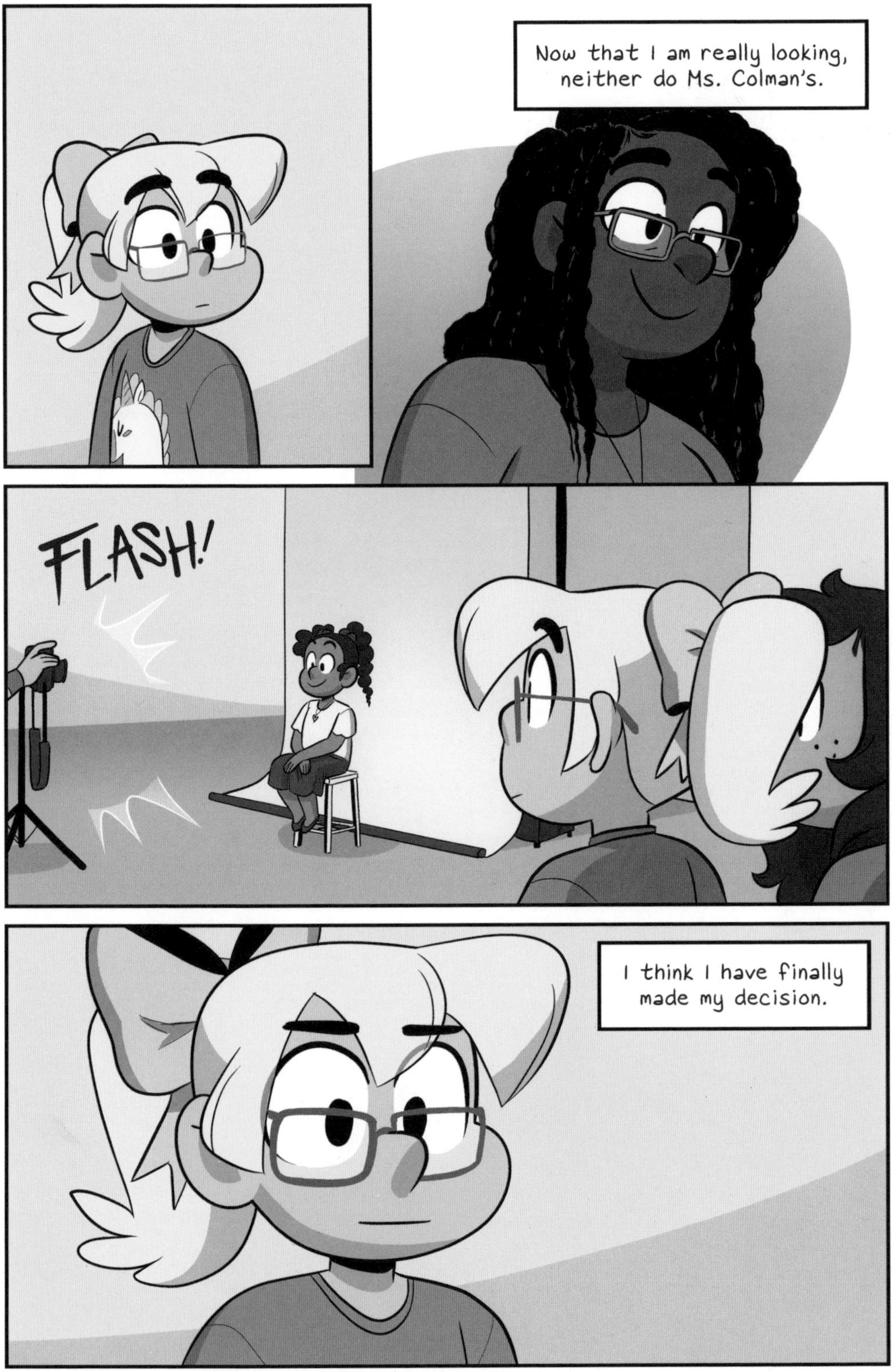
Now that I am really looking, neither do Ms. Colman's.
FLASH!
I think I have finally made my decision.

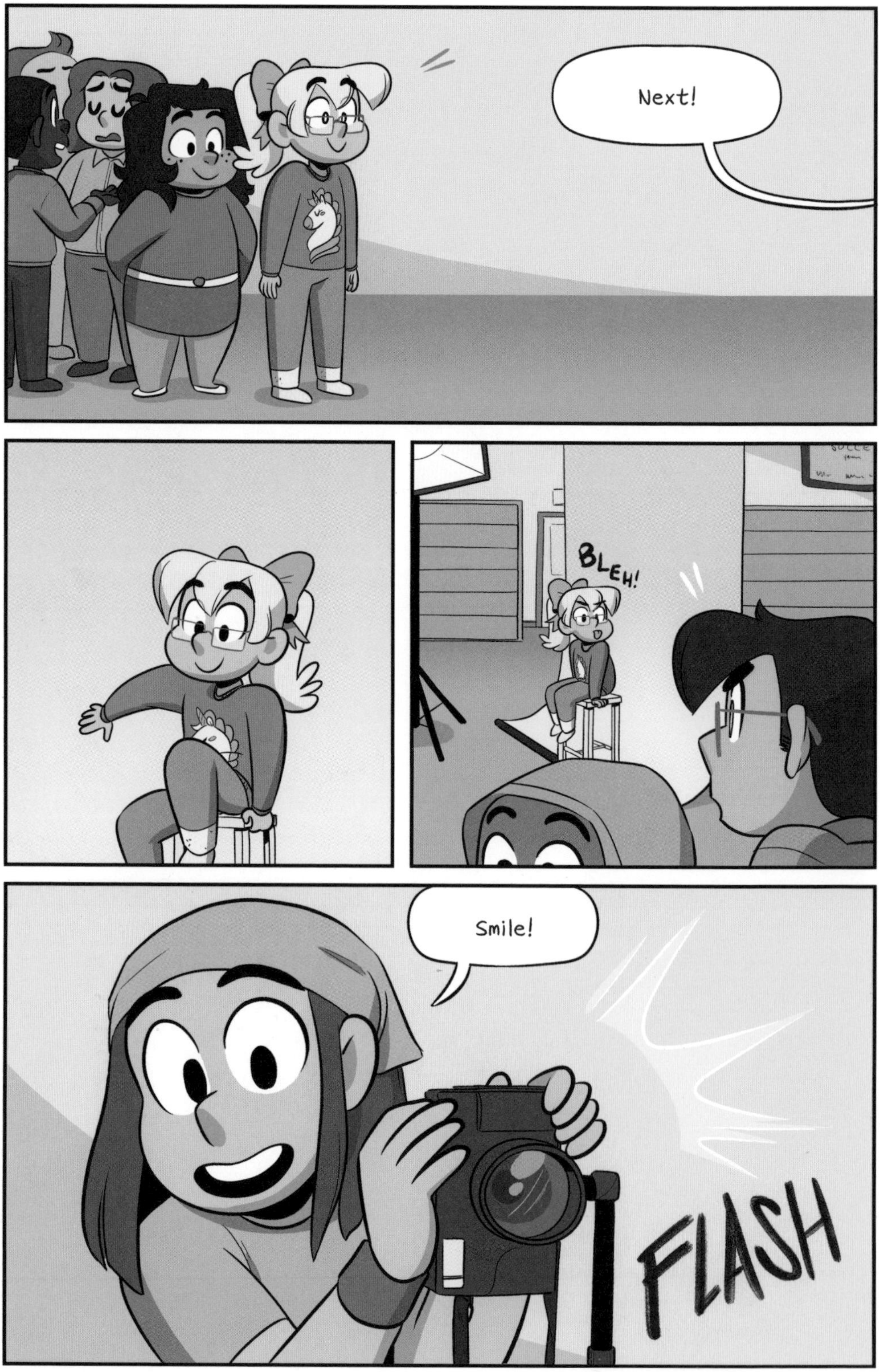
Next!
BLEH!
Smile!
FLASH

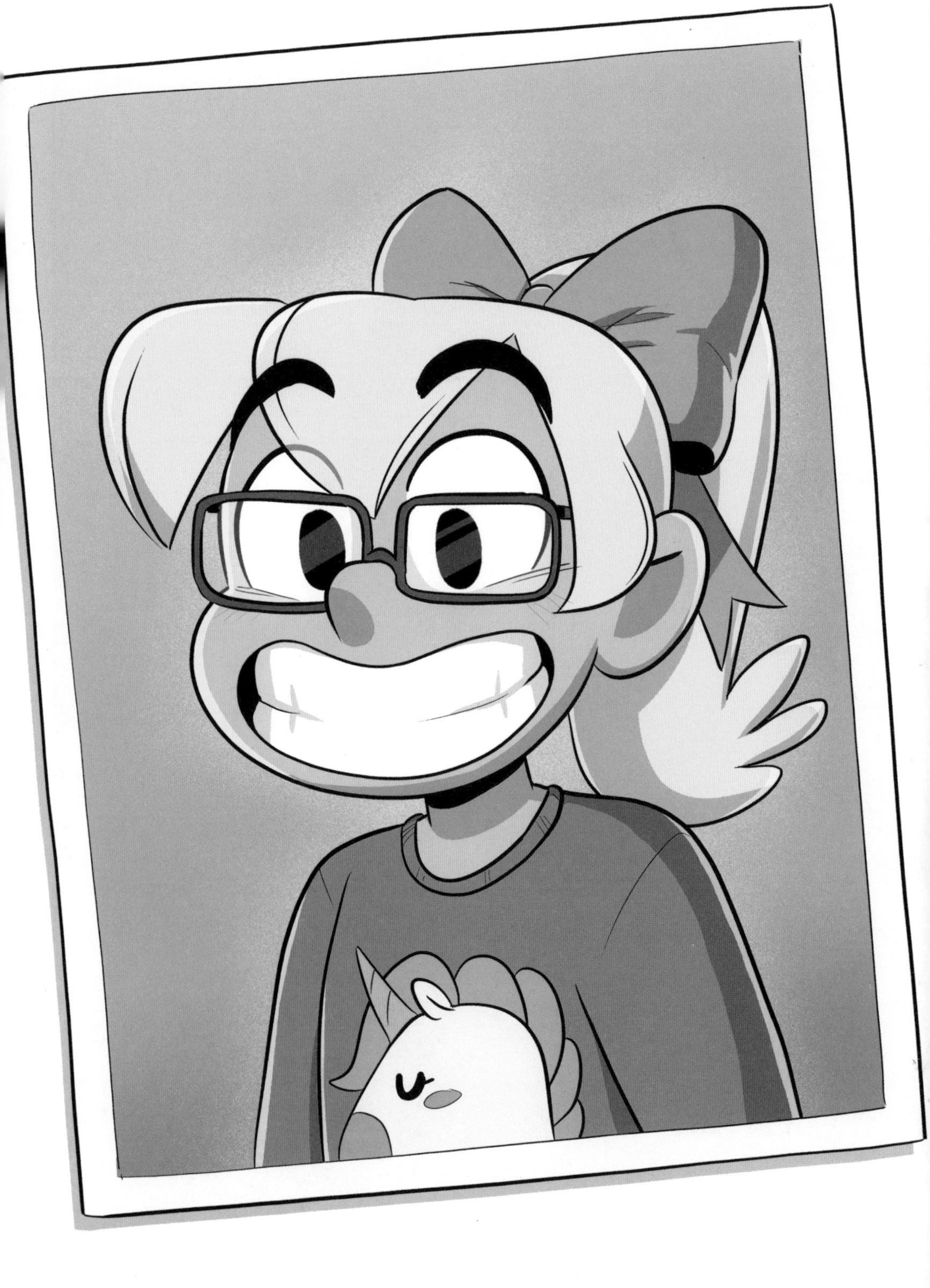

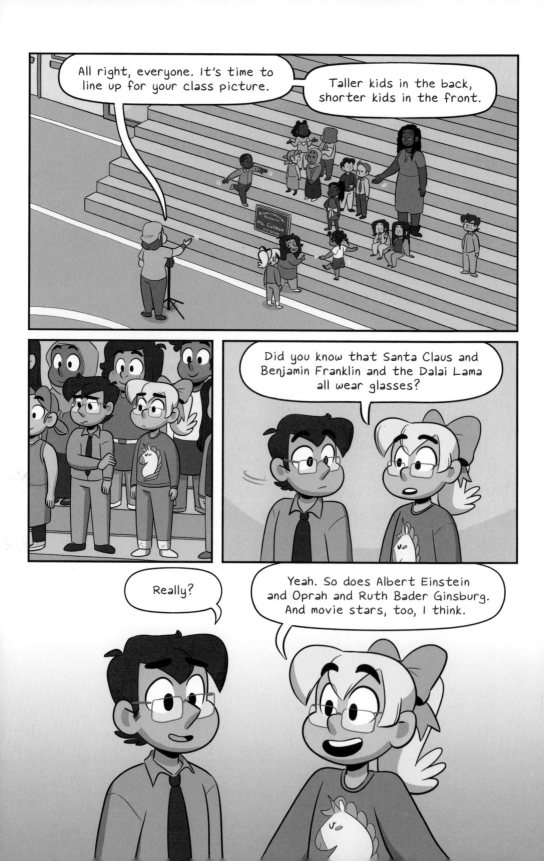

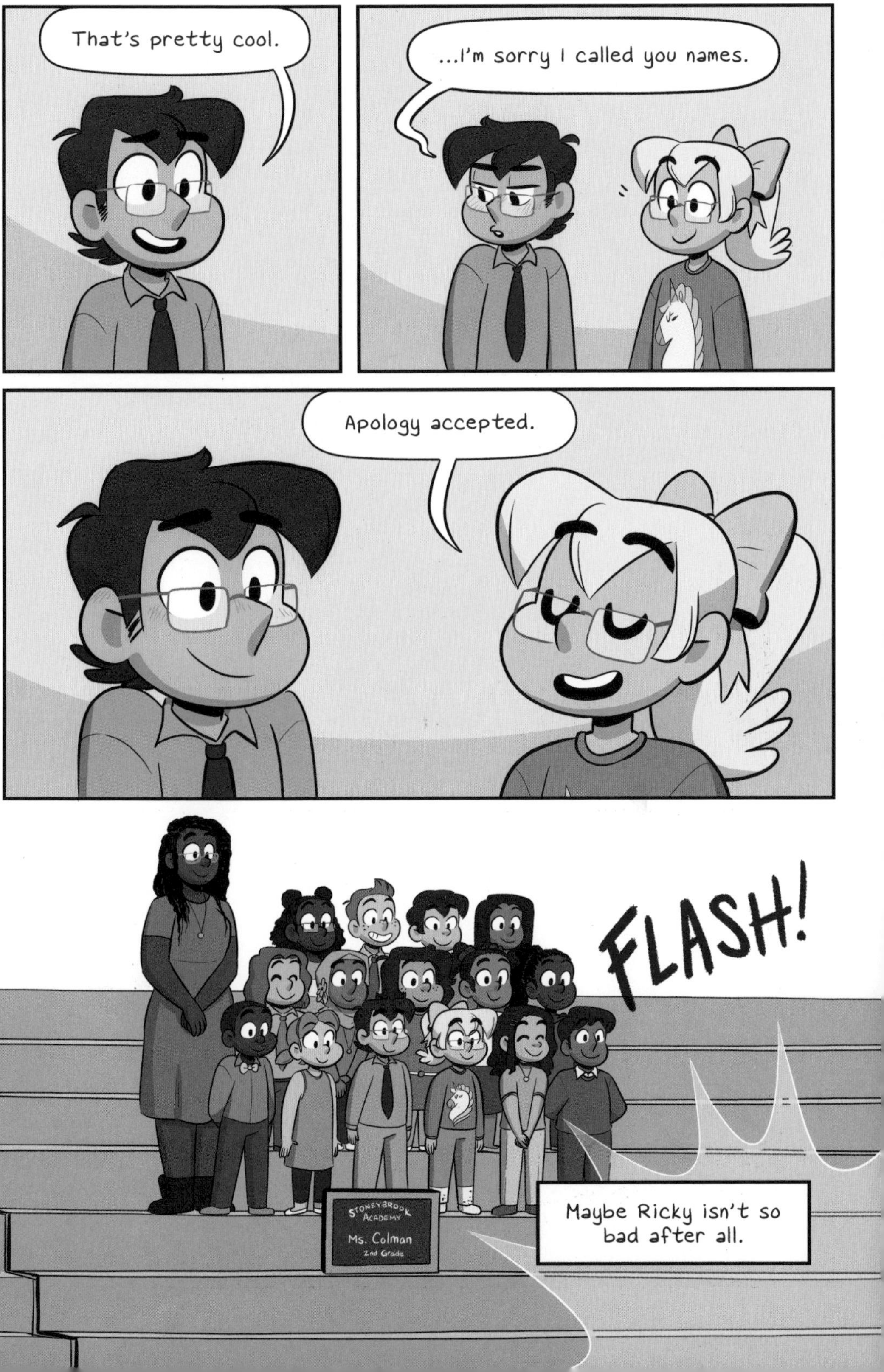
That's pretty cool.
...I'm sorry I called you names.
Apology accepted.
FLASH!
STONEYBROOK ACADEMY
Ms. Colman
2nd Grade
Maybe Ricky isn't so bad after all.

CHAPTER 10

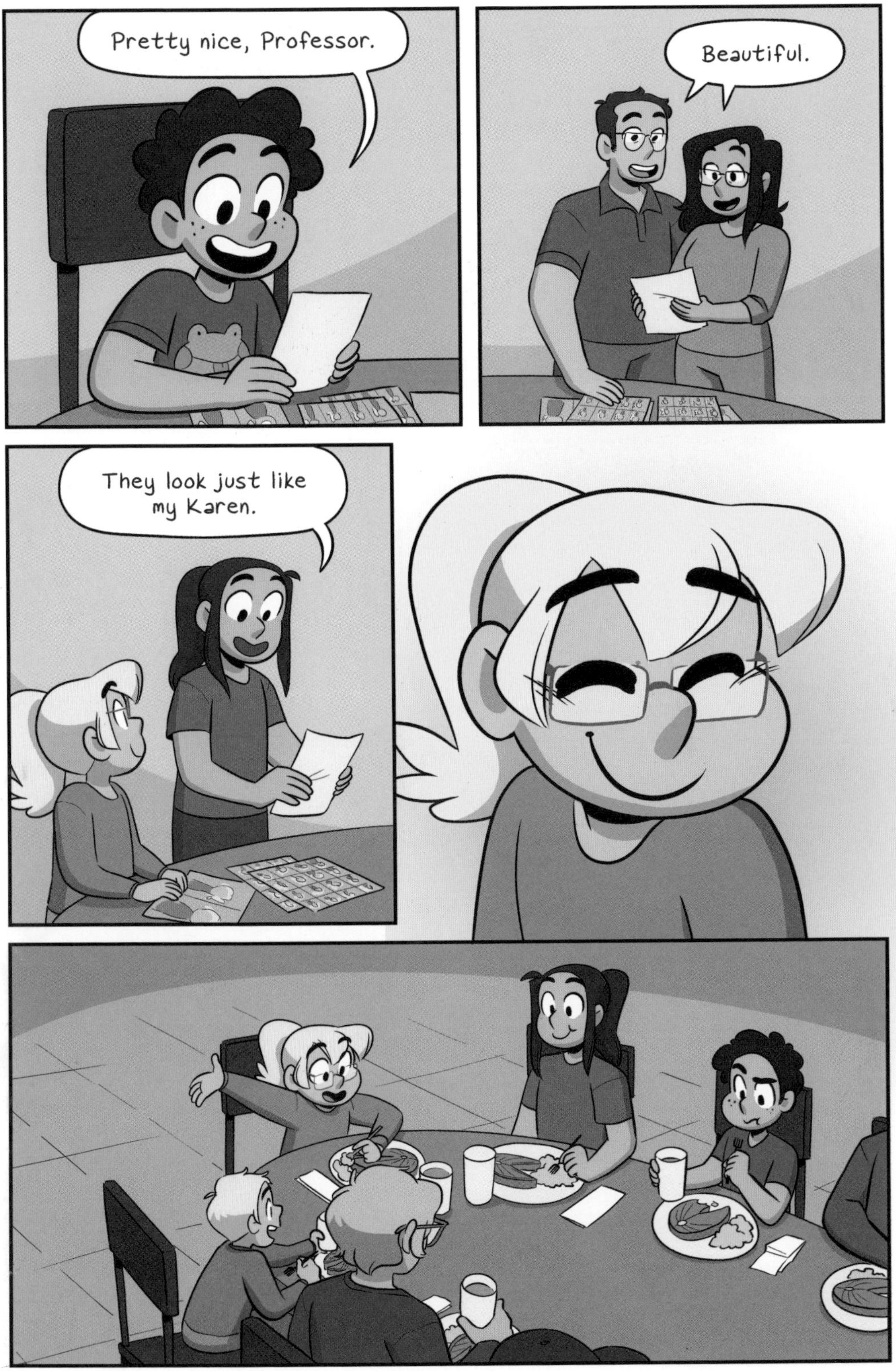
Pretty nice, Professor.
Beautiful.
They look just like my Karen.

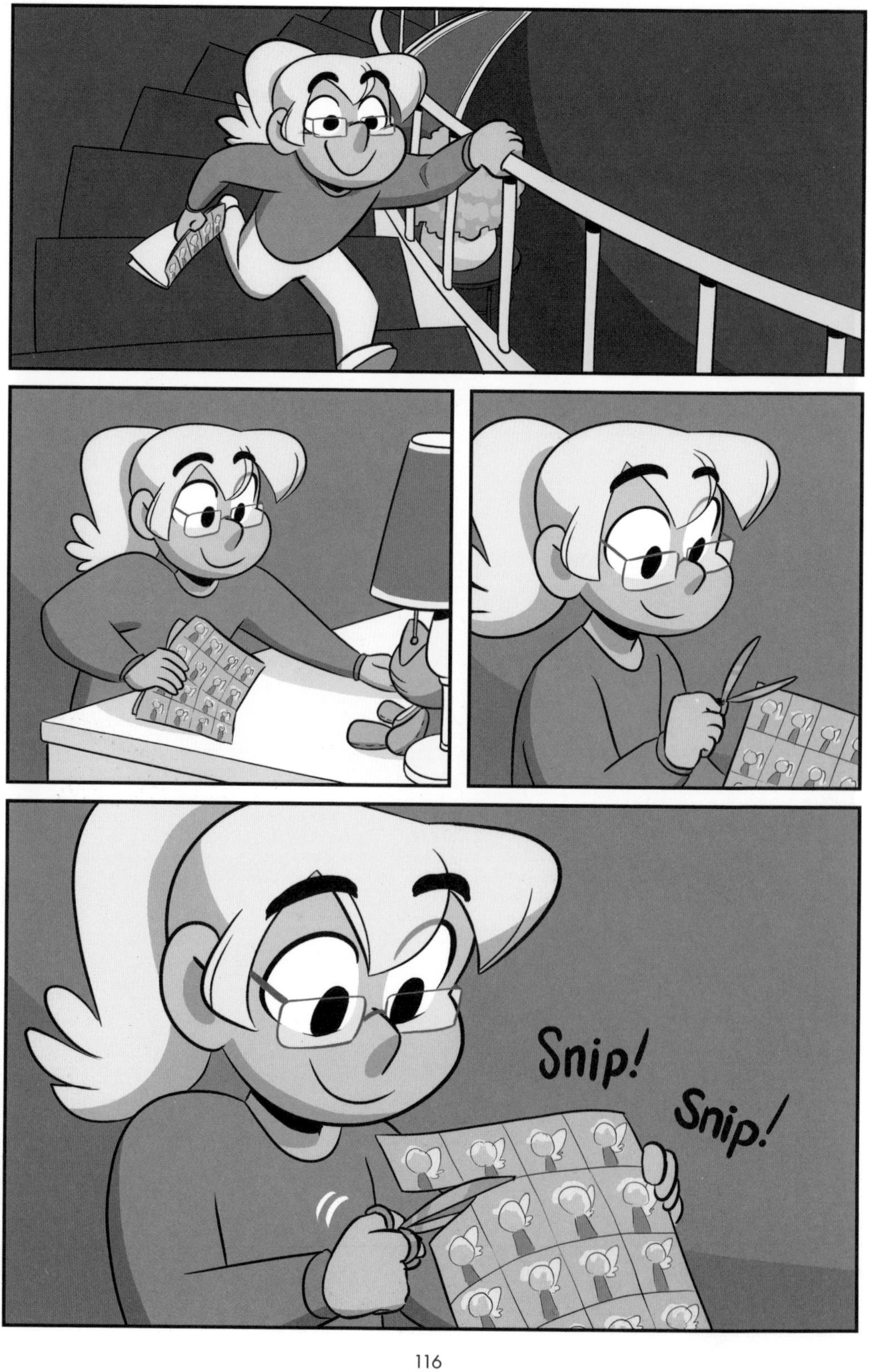
Snip!
Snip!

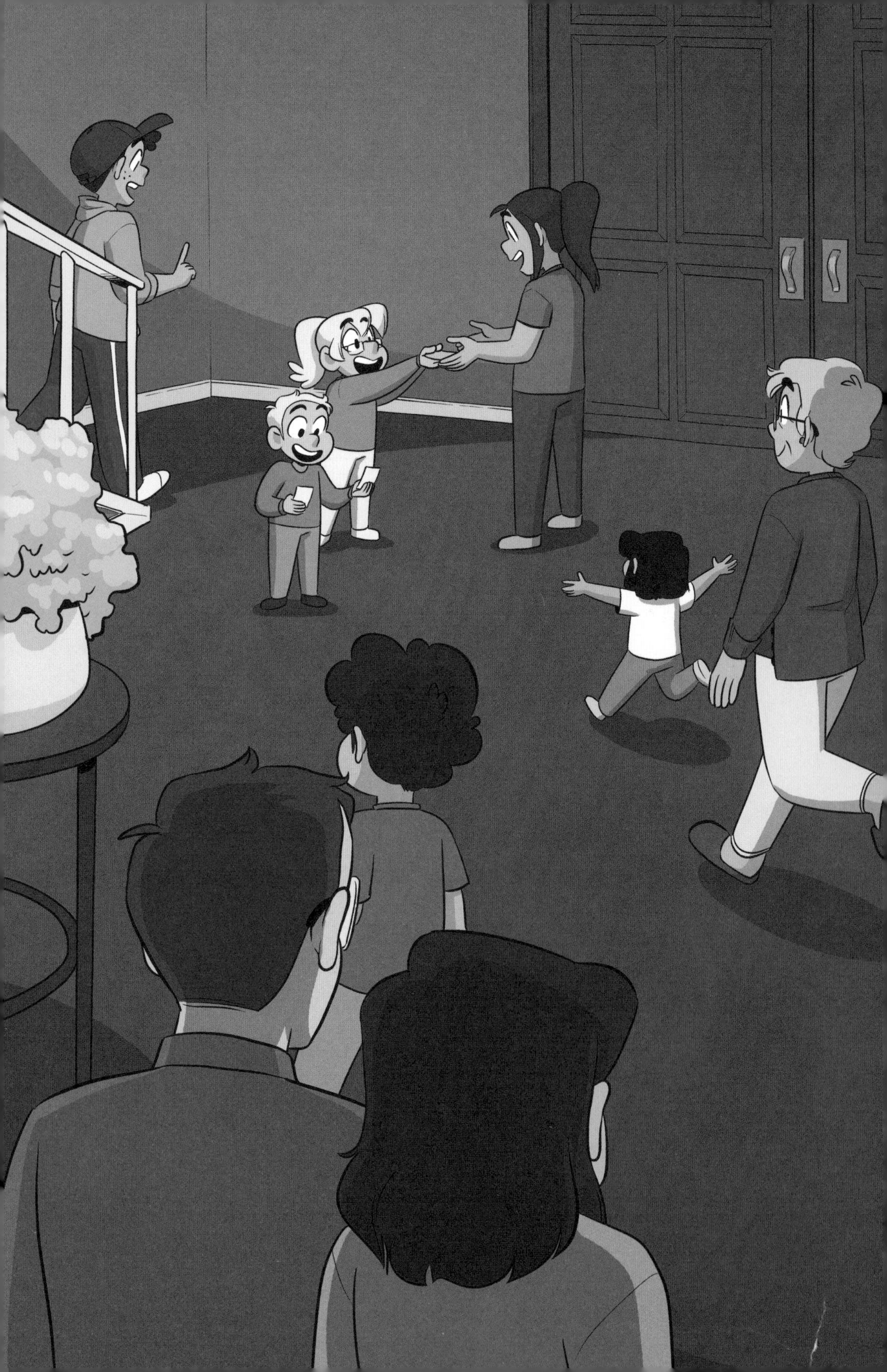

KATY FARINA is the creator of the *New York Times* bestselling graphic novel adaptations of the Baby-sitters Little Sister series by Ann M. Martin, and of an original graphic novel for young readers, *Song of the Court*. Previously, she painted backgrounds for *She-Ra and the Princesses of Power* at DreamWorks TV. Katy lives in Los Angeles with her husband and two rambunctious cats. Visit her online at katyfarina.com

DON'T MISS THE OTHER BABY-SITTERS LITTLE SISTER GRAPHIC NOVELS!

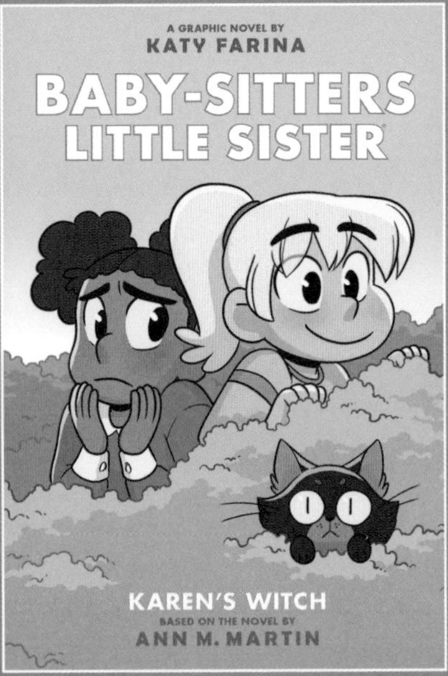
A GRAPHIC NOVEL BY
KATY FARINA
BABY-SITTERS LITTLE SISTER®
KAREN'S WITCH
BASED ON THE NOVEL BY
ANN M. MARTIN

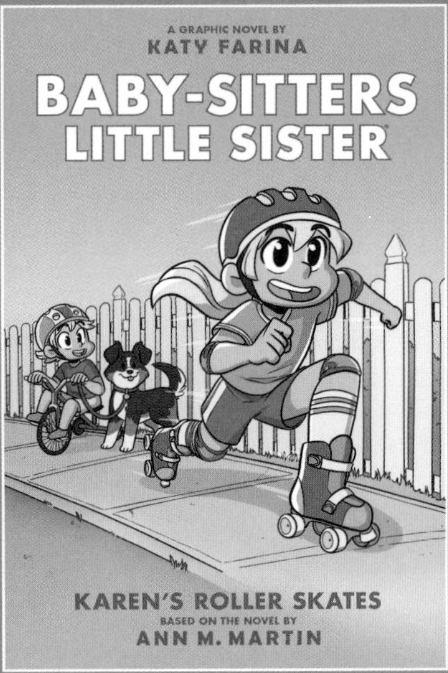
A GRAPHIC NOVEL BY
KATY FARINA
BABY-SITTERS LITTLE SISTER®
KAREN'S ROLLER SKATES
BASED ON THE NOVEL BY
ANN M. MARTIN

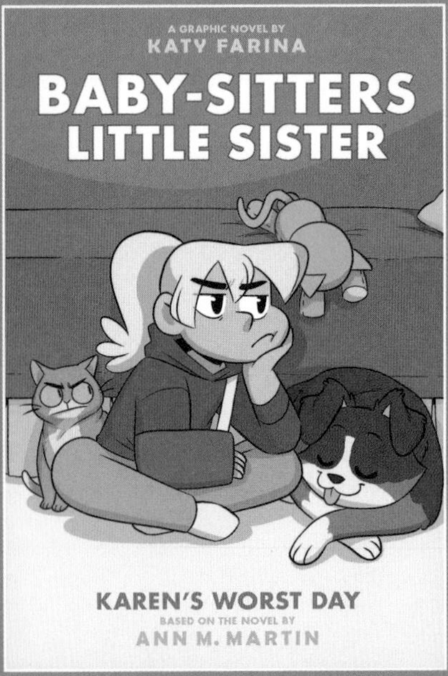
A GRAPHIC NOVEL BY
KATY FARINA
BABY-SITTERS LITTLE SISTER
KAREN'S WORST DAY
BASED ON THE NOVEL BY
ANN M. MARTIN

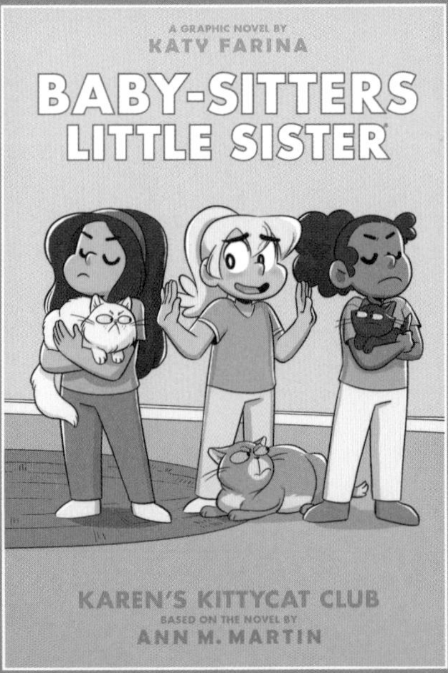
A GRAPHIC NOVEL BY
KATY FARINA
BABY-SITTERS LITTLE SISTER®
KAREN'S KITTYCAT CLUB
BASED ON THE NOVEL BY
ANN M. MARTIN

85